# CHAPTER 1 - TIME FOR A BREAK

It had been a long and grueling year for Charlie. He was continuously working overtime and taking on extra assignments from his supervisors. There was no time to party on the weeknights or take any trips on the weekends. He felt that he was burning out.

Charlie decided that he was going to put everything on pause and go on an exotic cruise trip for spring break. He didn't care about project timelines, milestones, or any future bonuses at this point. It was time to let it all go for once.

He browsed various cruise lines and looked for something at least a week long in duration and in a tropical climate. There was a seven-night cruise trip from Fort Lauderdale, FL to the Grand Caymans with other port stops at the Bahamas, Costa Maya, and Cozumel, MX. This was it! Charlie's Spring break and his first and only cruise trip. He setup his out of office responses for work and initiated hold mail for his residence. He assembled some relaxing swimwear, t-shirts, shorts, and shades and then picked out his plane flights to Florida. *Let the adventure begin!*

The next weekend Charlie was underway onboard his first ever cruise! His parents never got around to much family trips when he was growing up and Charlie was very much a dedicated bookworm. Getting out and having fun was extremely foreign to him. He was an all work and no play kind of guy. Since this was his first cruise, he decided to document everything! He took pictures of his sea-side cabin, the rich food and drinks, and more drinks, the pool deck, the seagulls flying along the breeze. Charlie was unbounded and free with no responsibilities for once.

After a few self-guided tours around the main deck Charlie made his way to the shore activity booth. To his surprise the ship's entertainment director was there in person talking directly to customers. *Wow this lady is like old and stuff to be the ship's entertainment director.*

"Hey there cutie, would you like to go on a tour with me?" She winked her eye at him playfully.

Charlie played along, "Baby I'm not good enough for a paradise adventure with you, but I'll take some of your information pamphlets if you don't mind."

She chuckled back, "Aww you're so sweet, I could eat you alive, but seriously Mr. what do you really want to do on this trip? It looks to me like you just want to party like the other spring breakers, not much for history or shopping."

"Um yes Ma'am, I 'm just trying to have as much fun as I can, this is really my first cruise trip and all."

"Well sweetie, most of the young adults I have seen on these trips tend to meet up at bars and then take it from there. It's usually the families with kids that go on these port tours, but since this is a 21 and up only cruise there aren't any kids onboard, a true booze cruise! If you're lucky you might even find yourself a cougar to befriend!" She winked at him again and then moved onto another customer. *There wasn't a single woman (young or old for that matter) that had paid any attention to him so far. He got a little confidence in himself, but not enough to strut his step with pride.*

Charlie grabbed a turkey sandwich from one of the many buffet stations and sat down near a couch overlooking the Florida coastline. As he ate, Charlie watched the ship pulling away towards the first port stop in the Bahamas. The coast looked like a sea of people invading the beaches. It was peak spring break season for the south. Charlie was glad he chose a less-chaotic trip and very much on cruise control.

He took one of the tri-fold pamphlets and raised it up to just about eye level. He leaned back on his lounge chair and looked back at the buffet line. He peered over the top and gazed out, people watching. A brunette there, then came a blond, then another brunette, another one, then a blond. Charlie didn't have a chance in hell with these gals, but it didn't stop him from imagining.

Before the evening came to a close Charlie went up to the pool deck and relaxed in a lounge chair, feeling the cool ocean breeze blowing over him while he drank a Mai Tai. He had attempted to swim in the pool but it was completely swamped with other spring breakers. People were literally smashed together like cattle and grinding it out half-drunk and full of hormones. While it did provide for amazing entertainment Charlie soon felt overwhelmed by the crowds and had to escape. The top deck overlooking the pool below was his oasis, his sanctuary from it all. He closed his eyes and thought about hooking up with some of the girls he saw throughout the day. *I can be funny and cool if I tried hard...or if I was drunk enough.*

Charlie blended in with the surrounding furniture like a fly on the wall and looked on at the sexual heat down below. He wasn't a strapping hot jock with killer abs or a funny personality. He was very much a loner. Perhaps he could go find a cougar and be her cub. The though of it was a little freaky in his head, but was probably going to be his best shot if he wanted to get laid.

He finished his drink along with some greasy pepperoni pizza. The unlimited food and beverage pass was dangerously good for this trip! Charlie had a nice buzz going and decided that he best get back to his own cabin. He took one last glimpse down to the pool deck and walked back to his cabin to close out the night.

# CHAPTER 2 - THE WOLF PACK

The early morning hours were all but forgotten as Charlie found himself trying to keep up with a small band of fellow spring breakers. They were all on their way to a coral reef snorkeling trip and it wasn't even Charlie's idea! He didn't even know these guys!

The man who dragged Charlie into this impromptu wolf pack was a an extremely well-built black dude called "Ray". Ray must have been a college athlete of some sort, which sport Charlie didn't really know, but Ray could talk your ear off and he seemed to be very smooth with the ladies in the bar as well.

Charlie was just trying to pace himself for the day with some ice water and a snack at the bar. He was trying to decide if he was going to swim with some beach pigs *(How was that a thing?)* or go on an ATV tour.

Then Ray showed up at the bar, saw Charlie and began to chat it up with him on the spot. Charlie was soon getting guy-counseled on the spot about his failures to have fun, let lose, and party hard like there was no tomorrow. Ray ordered several shots of Tequila and then challenged Charlie to drink with him. More shots of various liquor continued to appear in front of Charlie. Then Ray called his other friends over, next thing he knew Charlie was with the "Wolfpack" and Ray was their leader.

The second guy in the group was holding up a tourist map of the Bahamas and was adamantly pointing and yelling in the direction for the guys to head to. He appeared to be drunk as well.

Brian was on his second cruise trip for the year and seemed to have mapped out all of the great spots for the wolf pack to visit. Similar to Charlie's experience, Brian had also been approached by Ray and partook in a drinking challenge. Brian and Ray then teamed up to find more guys to create their adventuring club of misfits.

The third member was John and he was a straight up party animal. Both he and Ray seemed to be like brothers with the exception that John was white, not as built, but still must have been another athlete on spring break.

Brian had pointed out a cool snorkeling gig that was bound to have some fine ladies in bikinis. The headed out towards their destination, stopping at every bar along the way. It was a Caribbean bar crawl, Charlie's first! *So much for taking it slow. At least I get to experience this cruise trip with some friends instead of being by myself. Not a bad for an introverted workaholic!*

After several more pit stops the group finally arrived at their snorkeling destination. Charlie almost thought that he was in heaven.

# CHAPTER 3 - LADIES IN THE HOUSE

There on the beach and next to a large catamaran boat was a group of ladies, several of whom he recognized parting on the pool deck last night! It seemed that both groups were going to be on a snorkeling trip together.

Ray and John, wasting no time, walked over to the ladies and immediately introduced themselves.

Brian and Charlie checked into the snorkeling trip and began applying sun screen, the whole time, watching Ray and John smooth talk and joke around with the girls.

*That must be how it's done. Be funny, be sexy, be cool...*none of his qualities of course.

Like a student watching a teacher in a lab Charlie observed the other pack members making a play wit their charms. Then Ray pointed over to Brian and Charlie and the girls started walking over.

*What the hell Ray?! Why did you just send them over it's not like I'm a fellow smooth talker!* Charlie's anxiety began to rise, but soon one of them introduced herself as Lauren and greeted both Brian and Charlie. The anxiety quickly dissipated and everything went back to chill mode.

Lauren appeared to be the leader of the girl squad and was a history major. She was a tall, thick white girl with long blond hair. Charlie found it hard to focus as she gently walked towards him, her bikini top barely holding in her breasts as they jiggled up and down.

Charlie talked with Lauren for a while and was excited to learn that she and the other girls were trying to find an ancient Mayan ruin on the ship's next stop in the port of Costa Maya. Apparently, Lauren had done some extensive research on local legends for this portion of the cruise. She wanted desperately to document any artifacts that she could find along the way, and she wanted to have fun in the process. It was spring break after all.

Just behind Lauren was an even bigger girl, a thick Redhead named Desiree. She must have been like six feet tall and her curves were to die for! Desiree was studying to be nurse in the medical industry. She seemed to be a little shy which Charlie felt was a bit odd for the giant BBW that he saw in front of him. Desiree saw Charlie staring at her and she smiled before he could quickly look away.

Then there was Tiffany, oh Tiffany! *Was there some gorgeous BBW photo shoot going on?* Tiffany seemed to be the exact same build as Desiree, but had light brown skin with extremely long dreadlocks hanging down her back.

Charlie new that he had a thing for big women, but he had never been so close to any of them before and both of these ladies were extremely attractive! Desiree and Tiffany had on just enough clothing to pass for a snorkeling trip.

Tiffany began to adjust her bikini bottom when she dropped her mask and snorkel right next to Charlie. As she bent down her massive butt cheeks almost busted through her bikini bottom as they squeezed and flexed the fabric. Charlie was staring in awe, dumbfounded at her massive ass. It was a monster ass indeed and he wanted so badly for Tiffany to accidently rub up against him when she bent over.

She finally picked up her gear and started walking over towards the waiting catamaran. All of the guys were watching.

Lastly, there was a gorgeous Latina named Reina that seemed to have just recently joined the group. She was the smallest of them all but had a nice curvy body and long black hair. Her eyes were brown and welcoming. Reina was studying in psychology and had a strong interest in human behaviors.

The two groups continued to socialize for a bit getting to know one another. The guides for the snorkeling trip had stocked their boat with plenty of snacks and drinks for al the riders. They knew how to keep the party vibe flowing. That was important around spring break season, especially for all the college folks who wanted nothing more than to drink and go wild. The lead guide motioned for everyone to get onboard and started removing the mooring lines.

# CHAPTER 4 - FIRST BASE

Charlie continued to survey this now larger group as the catamaran headed out of port. Everyone had taken up social spots around the boat. Ray and John were completely flirting with the ladies talking about their favorite sports and hobbies that they were all so good at. *Must be nice to be an all-star athlete.*

He spotted Brian off to the side by himself. Brian was also people watching, but mostly person watching as he seemed to be staring at Reina with the other girls. Occasionally Reina would mess with her hair, run her hands through it or flip it a she talked. This seemed to get Brian's attention. Charlie got the sense that Brian wasn't a jock either.

So far, this trip was beyond amazing. In no possible way did Charlie ever believe that he could be in this situation with these strangers now turned friends, even if it was only for a short spring break vacation. Charlie then found himself looking over at Desiree. To Charlie she was like a woman from the amazon, or maybe a Nordic maiden. His mind went wild with imagination as he continued to watch her from afar.

Still, he was not very confident in chatting with the girls and as if on que here comes Ray, smiling with his dark shades and holding two large drinks, clearly some type of alcohol.

"Listen dude, you know this trip is about chilling out! I see you over there looking at them girls and I know you are interested. Hell we all are! I tell you what man, drink this shit up and come join us. They ain't gonna bite ya man! C'mon over!"

*Damn you Ray.  Making him leave his comfort zone again.*  At least Ray brought him a drink to help calm his nerves.

Charlie sat down next to Brian who also seemed to have been yanked from his perch and had a drink in his hand.  He looked up at Charlie and the two of them laughed.  Yes it seems they were both learning to chill. Ray really had a thing for getting people together.

John and Tiffany seemed to be getting along well talking about their favorite foods and club spots.  Ray was chatting with Lauren and asking for more details about the Mayan ruins.  Reina and Desiree had gone to get refreshments and came at the same time, each with two drinks.

They sat down so that Reina was near the outside, next to Brian, and Desiree was on the outside of Charlie.  Desiree slowly got down and then slide a little bit closer to Charlie, her thighs slightly touching his.  Charlie was now sandwiched in between Reina and Desiree.  He looked over to spot John gulping down his beverage and staring at Charlie.  He gave Charlie a quick wink and then resumed chatting with Tiffany.

Ray was also staring with the biggest smile ever and nodded his head slightly.  They were all enjoying taking in the sights and sounds of the catamaran trip out to sea.  The cool vibe was building, along with the buzz from the alcohol.  Charlie became chill.

With a little under an hour, they reached their snorkeling destination and got into the warm Caribbean water.  It was crystal clear, full of corals and tropical fish.  There were all types of bright and colorful species and Charlie recognized a few of them.  He knew about clown fish and blue tangs.  He also saw plenty of parrot fish and a few nurse sharks hiding within the corral.  The reef was vibrant with life, schools of fish would swim buy and school together in different directions with the sun's rays reflecting off of their scales.  One of the tour operators stated tossing out breadcrumbs around the boat.  The fish responded by swarming the whole area around the boat.  The girls were initially swimming together by themselves, but immediately made a beeline to the guys when the swarming began.

Soon the girls and guys were now swimming all together in one group. John, the jokester that he was, scared a few of the girls by swimming behind them and tapping them when they least expected it. This in turn caused a few friendly water splashing battles between the group.

So much horseplay seemed to be attracting more fish then scaring them, away. Suddenly Charlie felt a presence behind him, a big one! This wasn't Ray or John playing jokes because he was staring at them.

He slowly turned with some anxiety and right in front of him was Desiree! She was still going forward at the time and swam right into Charlie. The contact may have only been for a few seconds, but it felt like minutes to him. Desiree's wild red hair completely covered his face like a shiny octopus and her whole body smashed into his small form. Her massive boobs momentarily cut off his view from the underwater world as his face disappeared into them.

It seemed that she was panicking form the swarms of feeding fish and didn't notice that she was swimming right into Charlie. She gasped in surprise and they both went to the surface.

Once on the surface, Desiree immediately wrapped her arms around Charlie and apologized for close lining him underwater. Charlie was already laughing off his minor panic attack, glad to see that his underwater monster was just one of the girls! The two were both laughing and smiling in relief.

Charlie then realized that he was holding onto Desiree and she was still holding onto him. She had him pulled in tight to her soft body as her melons smooshed up against his chest. Then he felt her legs and hips wrap around his. Charlie immediately became aroused and just as he was about to panic again Desiree grabbed the back of his head and pulled him in for a deep French kiss. Her other hand went down into his swim trunks, feeling up his full erection. Then she released Charlie and continued snorkeling.

*Wow that was intense and amazing!* Desiree literally wrapped him up and made out with him in the water! She was clearly interested in Charlie, hell there might even be a chance that he was going to be laid in the future!

A loud whistle began to sound and Charlie looked over at the tour boat to see one of the guides shouting. The guide was yelling for everyone to get back on the catamaran immediately. Upon hearing this Charlie quickly swam back to Desiree and motioned for her to surface because she was underwater and did not hear the announcement. Then they joined the rest of the group in the water and got onboard the boat.

Brian spoke up first and asked what was wrong and why they had to get out of the water. He didn't see any sharks. A crewmember then held up a spear and pointed it down the side of the catamaran. Everyone peered into the crystal-clear water.

Down near the base of the closest coral bed and slowly rising from the bottom was a massive Goliath Grouper. It was almost the size of either Desiree or Trina! Its giant gapping mouth was filtering out water and completely open. It looked big enough to swallow a human whole! Well not just any human but perhaps a small adult and definitely a kid! The grouper continued to swim towards the catamaran and the one guide splashed his spear in the water...it kept coming. "Feet out of the water we are leaving!" Shouted the guide and the catamaran was quickly underway, returning back to the beach.

Everyone on the boat was talking about this monster grouper. Everyone except for Charlie. He actually had the best view when it happened, as he was the last person to back into the boat. He thought about what it would have been like to get swallowed whole and alive inside of that monster. Not that it would ever happen, but the thought of it kept going around in his head. *That grouper could have swallowed someone and then swam away, with no chance of rescuing its victim.* The guides tried to calm everyone down and explained that this one Goliath Grouper was known to be aggressive and that worst case it would have just nipped at the swimmers. They all then ordered another round of drinks and laughed away the whole experience.

When the catamaran was pier-side they got off and regrouped on the beach. It was agreed upon that they would all exchange phone numbers and hang out for not just the evening but the entire cruise trip. They shared each other's contact information and also took group photos for their social media posts. Back at the cruise ship folks split up and went their separate ways to prepare for the evening. It was going to be a club night!

Charlie proceeded back into the cruise ship from the main deck and walked towards his cabin. He paused and looked back out at the tropical beach. This paradise, the seagulls flying by, the other spring breakers storming the town and having the time of their lives. He was having the time of his life and he never expected it. He smiled again knowing that he had a fun group to hang out with for the rest of the trip.

He passed by several more girls, none of them either smiled or acknowledged his presence. Guess it was back to reality, being a loner, a non-interesting guy, wait a second! Then his mind flashed back to the moment when Desiree was making out with him in the water. *Damn I've already scored first base with Desiree!*

Everything was fine again, and almost on que Ray texted the group and said that they were going to eat at a local seafood restaurant in a few hours before clubbing. *This is life indeed!*

Just before he entered his cabin Charlie noticed an older gentleman laying in a lounge chair on his cabin balcony watching over the beach. He saw that there was some horizontal motion going on near his...yep, he was masturbating and scoping out the crowds below. Charlie was about to say something then stopped short before he could talk. *Why should I interrupt him? It's Spring Break after all and there is probably a couple of older women and men onboard that are getting off with all of this eye candy. I wonder if any of the cougars on board are getting off masturbating to me? Probably not.*

# CHAPTER 5 – DINNER IS SERVED

The group met up at the seafood joint Ray had mentioned and sat down in the beachside patio. Almost as if it was planned, each of the girls appeared to sit right across from the guy they had been hanging out with the most.

Ray and Lauren were getting deep into the historical discussion of the Mayans while Brian and Reina shared their likes of varying dance moves. Of course, John and Tiffany were talking all about the food menu. Desiree and Charlie were not as vocal, but continued to chat up about the snorkeling trip.

Desiree was telling Charlie all about her nursing education and how it was keeping her up late at night. Her studies forced her miss out on parties and fun events because she was constantly memorizing drug treatments and scientific names on every aspect of the human body. Charlie responded with his degree and how he too was locked down with studies.

Desiree smiled and moved some of her long red hair away from her blouse. Charlie was awestruck and staring directly into her exposed cleavage. It seemed like it was inviting him in for an encore hug! Desiree giggled and disrupted his stare. Then she took off her sandals and began feeling up Charlie's legs with her feet. She licked her lips and winked an eye at him while nobody else watching. Charlie felt his light pole hardening underneath the dinner table. He began to take some deep breaths as Desiree continued staring directly at him with a lustful gaze.

Everyone continued to chat and drink for a while and then one of the waiters brought in a huge fish, carved up and accentuated with herbed butter and some salad. Lauren then looked at Ray and gasped, spilling white wine all down her shirt and yelled, "Ray! You didn't!"

"Yes, yes, I did!" He was laughing so hard that he almost fell out of his chair.

John looked over and asked, "What type of fish is this?"

The one waiter responded, "Atlantic Grouper".

Everyone's eyes opened wide open in shock…except Ray.

Ray had now fallen out of his chair and was rolling around laughing his ass off! John started to laugh, and then Lauren, and then everyone else. They began talking about the monster grouper.

"Honestly, I would much rather be swallowed whole by something on land, like an anaconda, at least someone would find my body." said Brian.

"Yeah, but they still wouldn't find you. Anaconda's have a very powerful digestive system that can even dissolve bone! Most of the prey a snake eats is completely absorbed with little waste." Commented Lauren. "At least with most constricting snakes the prey would be completely incapacitated or suffocated before taking a trip down the hatch!"

Then John interjected with his comments, "Hey why are we talking so much about getting eaten? It looks to me like we are the ones doing all of the eating right now. Right?"

Then it was Desiree's turn to go all medical, "The air inside most creature's stomach doesn't have enough air for the prey to survive. If it wasn't torn to pieces or suffocated before getting swallowed, they prey would surely perish before the digestive enzymes would come into play."

For a minute the friends all went silent and then erupted into laughter. They were truly a squad, a team, and the adventure had just begun! The checks came around and the guys all paid for both themselves and their dates.

When Charlie paid for Desiree, she rubbed her foot seductively inside his thigh getting his attention.  He looked up to see her bring a big piece of grouper up to her mouth.  She tongued it, and then moved it around in her mouth slowly before swallowing it down with a big gulp.  Then she licked her lips and whispered to Charlie with a wicked smile… "I think I want to eat you, Charlie."

# CHAPTER 6 – LIVING IT UP IN THE CLUB

After dinner Brian had steered the group to a nearby dance club and bar.  As predicted the place was raging full of partyers.  They saw whip cream costumes, girl on girl wrestling, mixed wrestling, and plenty of drunk fighting.

As usual, John was flirting with every girl in the club. Tiffany was becoming visibly upset the more she watched him try and smooth talk his way around.  *Did John not get the memo that both he and Tiffany were dating?* Charlie watched the two argue near the bar for a bit then John stormed off into the dance floor.

Desiree saw the argument as well and told Charlie that they should go sit next to her and cheer her up.  They walked over and sat down next to Tiffany who was visibly crying over John.

"You shouldn't trust your heart to any one guy you meet on Spring Break Tif", said Desiree.  She told her that John was clearly a player looking out only for himself.

Charlie nodded and gave a few comforting words, "Yeah Tif, I know exactly what you are feeling, the rejection, the betrayal.  It had happened to me before when I first attempted to date back in high school.  In fact I never really got around to dating again until now."  *Was he actually on a date with Desiree?*  He seemed to be speaking this aloud from his heart and didn't realize it.

Tiffany whipped away her tears and told Charlie, "Well I think you are on a date honey".  She looked over at Desiree who also had a smirk on her face.

Desiree got up and sat down on the other side of Charlie. She leaned over with her large boobs pushing up from the table and looked back over to Tiffany. The two of them were staring at each other and nodding their heads. Desiree broke eye contact with Tiffany and looked down at Charlie's crotch for a brief moment with her eyes and licking her lips. *What is going on here?* He looked back at Tiffany who was smiling.

Tiffany got up and sat down on the empty barstool that Desiree just left. Then both Desiree and Tiffany scooted in real close so that their hips were squishing up Charlie between the two of them. Charlie felt his sides gently compress into the soft bodies of the girls. He could even smell the perfume that they were wearing. Desiree had some type of vanilla and cinnamon sent while Tiffany smelled like roses. Soon both of the girl's chests joined in with their hips as they sandwiched Charlie.

Without any warning both Desiree and Tiffany began kissing Charlie's ears and face. Desiree on the left and Tiffany on the right. The bartender approached to ask if they wanted a drink and saw that they were all pre-occupied so he let them be and moved on to some other spring breakers.

Ray, apparently watching it all unfold from afar, temporarily interrupted the action. "He'y yall, it looks like Charlie might be getting a little cold. Here take this beach towel to keep him warm." Ray winked his eyes at the girls and then walked away. Charlie reached out for the towel, but Tiffany grabbed it first. She unfolded the towel and placed it over Charlie's lap.

"You heard him Charlie. We gotta keep you from getting cold. Now sit back and let us warm you up."

Tiffany then went in for it and began French kissing Charlie. Charlie looked to his side nervously at Desiree who just smiled and then went down towards Charlie's crotch. Her head disappeared underneath the beach towel. Charlie felt her unzipping his pants. He nervously tried to pull away from Tiffany, but she pulled Charlie's face back to her wet mouth and tongued his whole face nice and slow.

Then Charlie felt a warm, wet, suction envelope his penis. Desiree was giving him a blowjob! Charlie was overwhelmed with wonderful sensations. He was sandwiched between two hot BBWs and they were making out with him, Desiree a little bit further. He looked up briefly to see that nobody cared at all. In fact, much of the club seemed to be in orgy mode. He let go of the tension in his body and surrendered to bliss.

Brian and Reina were tearing it up at the dance floor. They were crammed together like a pack of sardines with the other spring breakers. Reina looked over at the bar and saw Tiffany and Desiree working on Charlie. She turned back around, grabbed Brian and started to dry-hump him into the crowd of girls around them! Soon the other pack of girls responded by taking turns grinding up their butts into Brian's groin. Off to the side one girl grabbed his head and leaned into nibble his ear while Reina started to kiss down Brian's neck. More girls showed up, pressing their bodies into both Reina and Brian. Their soft curves only restricted by the super thin fabric of satin clubbing material or bikinis. Brian eventually realized that he wasn't dancing anymore, rather his body was being squeezed and smothered over and over again by the mob of wild girls.

Back at the bar, Desiree had progressed to deep throating Charlie. Her lips effortlessly glided all the way down to the base of his shaft as his the tip of his penis squeezed down her throat. She would suck hard and assault his shaft with her wet tongue repeatedly. *So this is what soul sucking is about.* He took note of the song playing in the background, Every Little Thing is Gonna be Alright from Aaron Neville. *Everything is definitely going to be alright! I could die right now and go to heaven!* Charlie felt that he was ready to pop. He tried to break free from Tiffany, as he didn't want to cum in her face.

Tiffany pulled Charlie back close to her body and then buried his head deep into her cleavage. She smooshed her boobs together, swallowing up his head into her massive cleavage. Tiffany's soft tit flesh cut out all of the light and muffled the noises in the club. The music playing in the background were songs from the Bob Marley and the UB 40 bands. Their smooth lyrics and base tones slowly melted all of Charlie's stress away as the girls worked him.

Charlie imagined himself getting lost between the girls, getting buried alive within their folds and never coming back from spring break. He had a thing for BBWs. Tiffany spit some warm saliva down her cleavage and let it drip all over Charlie's face. It glided in-between his face and her breasts like a warm lubricant. This new feeling combined with Desiree's powerful deep throating took Charlie over the edge and he popped.

Desiree clamped down all the way with her mouth and swallowed load after load of Charlie's hot cum down her throat. Tiffany could hear his muffled moans in-between her boobs and slowly smashed them together as hard as she could for a few seconds. They sealed Charlie in complete darkness and void of air while Desiree continued sucking away. It made Charlie climax one more time and both girls rode out his muscle spasms. Desiree emerged from under the towel and gat buck up on her barstool with a huge grin at Charlie. They ordered another round of drinks. Charlie definitely wasn't cold anymore.

On the beach nearby the club, combatants were furiously trying to wrestle each other into submission. The fights weren't violent in anyway, but physical, very physical, and sexually charged.

Lauren was very much an even match for Ray. He had no idea that this tall blond history major had any wrestling experience. She was holding her own against his attacks. Ray was just trying to have some hot and heavy fun. He was really beginning to like Lauren. Ray had almost pinned her down several times but she would easily slip away thanks to coating of honey all over her skin.

The honey was everywhere. Ray felt it all over his body down his underwear, on his face, up his nose. Lauren had smothered Ray several times with her boobs earlier in the match when Ray "Let her" take him down.  Now he wanted to try to wrap up this fight with a win.

Lauren was knew that Ray was much stronger, but she seemed to have better awareness of her surroundings.  She caught eye of a large patch of slick honey near the edge of the mat and backed into it.  Ray followed her. Then Lauren backed behind it and carefully stepped over the honey while simultaneously wrapping up Ray and pulling him towards her.

Ray's feet then hit the honey and he quickly fell down.  Lauren, still holding onto Ray smoothly slid right on top of him straddling his waist. "Better tap Ray!" said Lauren.

She slid her thighs right up to the sides of his head and then shoved her pussy right into his face! She was queening him! Lauren rolled her eyes up and gasped in excitement as she felt Ray's face get smooshed deep into her cunt.  She began to rock back and forth using Ray's face as a fuck toy.  Ray, half excited, half still in shock let Lauren hump his face for a short bit before he got his one hand free to tap out.

Lauren, clearly beginning to orgasm, wasn't paying attention to Ray's hand gently tapping her thigh. She continued grinding on his face.  Ray began to wonder where the referees had gone or if there were any in the first place. *Isn't anyone gonna stop this?* He began to drift in and out of consciousness. He felt Lauren's soft vaginal lips pressing hard into his nose and mouth through her panties while the back of his head was rubbing against the wrestling matt beneath him.  Lauren pressed down with more of her body weight into her bucking hips.

Ray began to lose hearing of the chanting crowd.  He couldn't feel his arms and legs anymore.  His vision began to fade out and the last thing he heard was Lauren climaxing with deep, guttural moans.

Through the orgasm, Lauren completely squeezed Ray's head into her hips and juiced hot cum through her panties all over his face. She shuddered for a little and screamed in joy to which the crowd all cheered. She then unmounted and got up. She looked down at Ray with a big smile. He was defeated and the whole section of the matt around his head was soaked in a mixture of the wrestling honey and her warm cum. Lauren teased him, "You're my bitch now Ray. You lost to my pussy. What are you embarrassed? You hear me? Ray?...RAAAAAY?!"

Lauren's facial expression changed from victorious to horror. Ray still wasn't moving. The crowd started to hush as well. Lauren began to tear up thinking that she smothered Ray to death!

She went back down to the matt and just as she was about to start CPR Ray came back to life coughing up some of her cum and the honey! He sat up in still in shock to what happened and said, "Wow that actually tasted kind of sweet!"

Lauren embraced him crying and apologizing. The crowd then went crazy now that they saw he was all right and moved on to watch the other combatants. Ray calmed Lauren down saying that he was going to be all right. He also said that it was one of the most intense matches of his life, literally! They both looked down at his crotch and saw his massive raging hard. Ray clearly loved the feeling of being dominated by Lauren! She balled her moth trying not to laugh as she stared at the wondrous sight and then hugged him again, carefully this time. They went down to the beach to wash themselves off and came back to the club to find the others.

Tiffany had ordered another round of drinks and told Desiree to make sure to "wash it all down." Charlie, still love drunk, watched Desiree guzzle down a margarita on the rocks, slosh some it around in her mouth and drink some more. The she swallowed more of it down and Charlie just kept staring at her as she did. Both Desiree and Tiffany now understood that Charlie was a virgin and they both chatted a little while making slight eye contact with him. Charlie heard bits of their conversation mainly, "he's so cute" and "we need to take him soon, but not tonight".

A group text popped up on everyone's phone and it was John

apologizing to the group for his behavior earlier. He said that he went back to the cruise ship to rest. He said not to wait up for him. It was past midnight and the ship was getting underway in the morning so they all left the club and headed back to the ship.

After John had sent the text, he set his phone on silent and placed it on the bed nightstand. He walked over to the college hottie that he spotted on the dance floor after his argument with Tiffany. John took another sip of his whisky and then began missionary fucking her in his stateroom. He had no loyalties with anyone and besides this trip was for himself anyways, no attachments, no strings, no commitments.

He railed the girl over and over while he thought things through. *Maybe I'll get around to hooking up with Tiffany again before the trip is over.* She did have one of the biggest pear-shaped asses that he had ever seen. He wanted so desperately to slide deep into that thick ass! As he thought more and more about it his dick built up to maximum pressure and came inside of the girl.

She squealed and yelled at him, "You're supposed to pull out before you blow MF!" "Fuck!" She put her clothes on and stormed out, probably to the ship's medical department for Plan B.

*Dumb fuck, what is she thinking having unprotected sex with people on spring break? What did she think was going to happen?* John then completely drank the rest of his whisky and passed out drunk.

# CHAPTER 7 - MISSION PLANNING

A loud vibration woke Charlie up and he popped up out of his bed with a surging headache! He looked down at his phone and it was Ray again group text inviting everyone up to the pool deck for brunch.

The party members slowly made their way out of their rooms and got ready.

When Charlie arrived at the pool deck, he saw the squad already assembled near the far end with a smorgasbord of breakfast selections. Ray, was the first to notice Charlie, as usual, and stood up to waive him over.

Charlie sat down and eagerly began to pick from the selection, a nice croissant, some eggs and bacon.

"Thanks, you guys for such a wonderful time," said Charlie.

Then they all cheered with some mimosas, followed by lots and lots of water. *Have to take it easy after last night.* They all agreed that the club was wild, to which Brian shook his head in satisfaction after recommending it. Everyone seemed happy and content. They talked about the next port visits and Lauren brought up her interest in the Mayan ruins again.

Reina noticed that John was not with the group and said, "Hey where is John at?"

All of the conversations stopped. Tiffany was about to say something and then everyone's phones got another group text. It was John.

"Hey everyone, I'm sorry for last night, would it be okay if I could still hang out?" The group then looked at Tiffany and sensed a little agitation.  Tiffany said that she didn't mind and John could do whatever the F he wanted.  She looked at Charlie and said rather seductively, "Besides, Desiree and I have a new best friend now."

Brian and Ray both shouted in joy and pointed at Charlie, but Desiree interrupted and said, "Hey we didn't go all the way...yet".

"All right all right that's enough people," said Lauren.

John finally showed up and walked around to Tiffany, but she said that the seat was taken.  "Bridge still burnt." thought John and he walked back and sat down next to Charlie.  Lauren then proceeded to tell the group about the plan for Costa Maya.

"Almost an hour away from the main coastline are the ruins of the ancient Mayans.  There are already several tour groups setup to go and see the popular ones, but I have done some research and..."

"And what?!" said Reina.

"And...there is lost Mayan ruin just a little further away that is not mentioned on any tour maps.  It appears to be mentioned as an unmarked temple area that the locals deter people from visiting."

 "That's extremely interesting," said Brian.  "Is there a chance that we might find some like treasure and stuff over there?"

"Yes, it's possible, but I'm really more interested in the ancient Mayan lore and mythology.  Rumor is that this specific temple may have been an ancient ritual site for a woman called La Xtabay. She was originally called Utz-Colel and competed in love in beauty with another lady called Xkeban.  Something happened, Xkeban died and the villagers buried her body with some extremely fragrant flowers.  Not to be outdone, Utz-Colel then vowed to die with beautiful smelling flowers because she was pure and did not sleep with the countless men of the village. Yet she died with the most wretched smelling flowers that anyone had ever smelled.  Later she prayed to come back to life as a woman to which she did, and she was extremely beautiful.  However, on the inside she was full of rage and with an eternally lustful and predatory heart. She would stalk any village men late at night, seduce them and then have sex with them. Then after completing sex, she would devour the men alive in the form of a giant snake! She looked like you Reina, long dark, black hair, but she would be in a white dress."

Reina's eye's opened in awe to Lauren's story as did the rest of the group.

John then blurted in, "Sounds like my kinda woman!"

Tiffany, still upset answered back, "Obviously I wasn't!"

Ray tried to cool things back down again, "Guys, guys, c'mon calm down. Hey we were all wasted last night and things happened man. Things happened. I know this aint' Vegas, but lets just move on and try this adventure please?"

Ray had a way of keeping everyone cool. He didn't really talk about what sport he played, but Charlie thought he might just be like the quarterback of a football team or perhaps some leadership position. Everyone finished eating their meals and agreed to get together again for tomorrow's shore party excursion to a forgotten Mayan temple!

The ship's announcement system came on and the captain spoke with an important announcement. "High everyone and I hope you are all having a splendid time on this Caribbean Cruise! I just wanted to let you know that we are currently tracking a tropical depression that just appeared in the Gulf of Mexico due East of our position. Now it's too early to tell if it's gonna build up to a hurricane and we don't know what path it will take, but we are still planning to dock in Costa Maya tomorrow. Worst case we might be in port for several days to wait it out and if needed we can plan refunds and travel compensation. Please enjoy your bright sunny day at sea with us and leave all the worries to us!"

As soon as the announcement had finished a huge argument erupted behind the friend's table.

"Fucking great! I've spent all this money on this damn trip, I've helped paid for your brat daughter to go to some dumb as college, and I have to work nights and weekend when we get back!  Why the fuck does this shit keep happening to me!"

"Jim please!  You're drunk again.  I'm certain we can get vouchers if anything gets canceled."

"Oh yeah vouchers for you and Amy!  You do realize that blackmailing daughter of yours has just been taking money away from you and me ever since I married you.  That's probably why your first husband left!"

"Jim stop!"

"I'm serious! You and her, are both eating me alive, milking me dry of all my money! Damn sugar daddies! I knew I should never have come on this damn trip!"

The group watched as the wife furiously left the table next to them, leaving the husband alone to finish his drink.

Charlie spoke up, "Ah shit I hope this doesn't mess up our plans for tomorrow.

"At least we will be in the same port as the ruins," said Brian.

Reina and Brian then went to go try their hands at some deck games while Tiffany, Lauren, and Desiree went back to their cabins to change into swim wear.  They were going to sun tan and chill at the pool deck all day.

John and Ray teamed up to go workout at the gym leaving Charlie explore the ship on his own.

When Charlie settled down in another lounge, he pulled out his phone and tried to browse the internet for any details on these ancient Mayan ruins near Costa Maya.  The internet connection was in and out but it was enough for him to get some information.

Apparently, the foul-smelling flower that Lauren had mentioned in the legend were actually emitted from the flowers of the Tzacam cactus.  The sweet smelling flower was supposedly some kind of morning glory commonly called Convolvulaceae and it climbed as a vine in the trees with white flower trumpets. There was also a large tree that this so-called angry female spirit inhabited or haunted. It was called the Ceiba tree and this Xtabay was all about this tree.

He browsed some more sites and then checked his personal email. Just a few messages from home, mainly his parents wishing him a happy cruise and hoping that all was going well at school. Then there were some more messages from a few colleagues at his school asking for help on class projects over the break. He completely ignored those. *I'm not trying to do any work on Spring Break! What is wrong with them?*

Later during lunch Charlie went to go try out different activities throughout the ship. He got into a comedy show, browsed some shops, and ate way too much food again.

His mind began to wander on Desiree. He thought of her ever since the snorkeling trip and he couldn't let her out of his mind, especially after last night. He eventually made his way back up to the pool deck to see if he could find her and yep she was, tanning with a very skimpy bikini.

Charlie thought to himself that he might be to annoying if he were to try and hang out with her and the others or disrupt her peaceful slumber. It's not like this trip was going to last very long and he felt that he should at least hang out with her on the pool deck if she would let him. So went to the bar, got two drinks, and approached her.

He nervously sat down and greeted her. She didn't answer, and her shades were on. *Well shit. I'll just leave this drink and get going then.*

As Charlie began to get back up Desiree yawned and saw him, "Hey Charlie".

"Oh hey Desiree I'm sorry I just saw you lounging around and got you a drink, but I'm interrupting your tanning session so I'll just."

She then grabbed his arm. "Hey can I borrow your hands for a minute please?" *Hell yeah you can borrow my hands.* Desiree then handed him a bottle of sunscreen and turned over.

Charlie started lathering her back, careful not to get into her privates. Then she unhooked her back strap to her bikini. Charlie lathered the lotion all over her back, down her hips and legs. Then he started on the back of her thighs.

She grabbed one of his hands again and guided it underneath her bikini bottom and right into her ass cheeks. She giggled and said, "Get in there Charlie. Get all in there for me."

His face now blush with embarrassment he did exactly as she said and thoroughly covered her entire backside. When he was done he sat back down next to her and quickly put a towel over his groin to hide his erection. Desiree turned her head to stare at him and smiled. Then she said, "Charlie, you're a keeper."

# CHAPTER 8 – WELCOME TO THE JUNGLE

It was hot, humid and the jungle was filled with the loud sounds of tropical birds attempting to compete for a mate or ward of predators. A strong seaward breeze was coming in from the coast. It was part of the approaching tropical storm in the Gulf of Mexico.

The friends had been searching for ruins for hours and they were all begging to think that they themselves were all lost. John was getting increasingly more frustrated that he had joined this lost expedition instead of finding more girls to screw on the beaches of Costa Maya.

He spoke up and said, "We should all just call it a day and head back before anyone gets hurt."

Ray quickly second the idea while looking at Lauren who was beginning to get frustrated as well. She couldn't spot any traces of the lost ruins beyond the obvious tourist ones close to the shore. They were all deep into the Jungle. The sounds of the crashing waves were all gone.

Reina and Brian seemed to be arguing about yesterday. It seems like she caught him hanging out with some other girls right after they had just hung out. She was clearly upset about it.

Tiffany was in the back with Desiree trying to keep up as both of them had a lot of weight to carry on the excursion (literally).

Suddenly Charlie smelled something awful and told everyone to wait up.  They all turned to see if he saw something.  He asked everyone if they smelled it as well and slowly but surely, they all did.

Lauren and Ray then began leading the group to this peculiar smell, cautiously looking out for any predators as it could have been the carcass from a freshly killed animal.

Once they got really close to the smell, they came across several cactuses with small blooming flowers.  Nearby was an oddly warped and tall tree.  It's tree trunk was huge with large deep roots.  Then Charlie remembered what he read about yesterday and told everyone it was a Ceiba tree and that the foul smelling stench was coming from the nearby Tzacam cacti.

Lauren shouted out in Joy, "Charlie those are both natural plants from the legendary Mayan mythologies! How did you know that?!"

Charlie responded back, "I guess I know a thing or two." He smiled for remembering and looked back at Desiree who smiled back at him.

They continued for a few minutes and Brian spotted what looked like part of temple staircase covered in dense jungle vegetation. He pointed it out to the group and everyone yelled in victory.

"I think we should setup bas camp right here, just in case something happens inside the ruins." Said Ray.

Lauren looked over at Ray and thanked him for being so thoughtful and supporting the expedition.  Then she turned around and thanked everyone, because they were truly acting as a team and now she was able to scour the ruins for any artifacts about Xtabay.

Ray then asked for volunteers and both John and Brian immediately volunteered to stay behind to setup base camp next to the Ceiba tree. *Well that was quick*, Charlie thought.  Then again, John seemed to just be hanging out only to screw Tiffany and he didn't really seem to like her.

Brian had proven that he wasn't necessarily tight with Reina either.  Maybe there was a chance that they would make it up somehow, maybe they would find some ancient Mayan treasurer and get rich!  The rest of the group then proceeded inside the ruins to see what they could find.

"This is stupid, honestly we are wasting our time on these ruins, it's just old history and we could be having so much fun on the beach proclaimed John."

Brian had no doubts the only reason John came back to the group was to try and score on Tiffany's thick "Georgia Peach Ass" as John would say.

"Hey man if you want to head back to the beach that's fine, I know this can be boring, besides we got some days here in port because of the storm in the Gulf.  You heard the captain this morning.  He said we are staying at least two full nights before getting underway again.  That gives you more time to score with Tiff if you want to."

John looked back at Brian in amassment.  *Had he really been that obvious about his intentions?  Guess so.*

"Hey man I would appreciate it if you just told them that I got bored or something and went back to the boat, not that I'm trying to score on Tiffany or anything."

It's cool bro, I understand, we are all trying to have fun on this trip.  Hey me and Rcina aren't necessarily tight either, there are some fine ladies that she introduced me to back at the club and I met up with them yesterday, so it is what it is man."

"Yeah man, it is what it is, hey I'll see ya later bro and thanks for understanding."

"Later bro."  Brian watched John back track to the beach again.  He felt like he should have joined him as well.  He remembered those girls in the club Reina introduced him to back in the Bahamas.  They were literally all around him, rubbing their asses and boobs all over his body.  *Hell it was Reina's idea to mix with those girls in the first place!* He continued to think about just leaving and following

John, he didn't want to be a jerk and abandon the other folks, but then again Reina was still upset with him and Brian wanted to just go and start fresh with another girl. He then picked up his stuff and began walking back to the beach.

Down in the Mayan ruins Lauren, Desiree, Tiffany, Reina, Ray, and Charles were exploring the dark passageways. They weren't prepared for dungeon crawling, had no protective gear, lighting, or even tools. They had to use their cell phones as flashlights to light the way.

Lauren looked at her watch and realized that they only had a few hours of sunlight left. She suggested that they all split up and search the various sections of the ruins for an hour and then head back to base camp with John and Brian. This would give them at least two solid hours of sunlight to help them leave the thick jungle and get back to the coast. They would then follow the coast back to the ship.

There were six of them in the ruins so they split up into 3 teams of two. Lauren and Ray, Desiree and Charles, and then Tiffany and Reina. The signal reception for their phones was very weak so Lauren stressed that no matter what all parties had to re-group at the base camp no later than the one hour of exploration.

# CHAPTER 9 – AN ANCIENT EVIL

Reina and Tiffany used their power hour to talk all about their experiences with their now absent partners. Reina vented about catching Brian with a bunch of girls last night by the pool deck and Tiffany raged on about how John only cared about her ass and nothing else. Both then began to talk about all the other guys they had seen on the trip and began to shit talk and vent non-stop. They were on a super girl-girl talk power hour. They were better the more and more they vented.

Then Tiffany mentioned Charlie's name and recalled how Charlie was actually a nice guy. She then told Reina about how she French kissed him and then held him captive smothered deep into her cleavage with a sexy bear-hug while Desiree was deep throating him!

"Now way!" said Reina. "Damn I wish I was there; I would have fucked him into heaven!"

They both laughed and then suddenly Reina tripped and fell down some hidden stairs and slid down into a hidden room. Just like that, Reina had disappeared. Tiffany was yelling out her name and searching desperately for Reina with her cellphone light. Her hands shaking, nervous and scared.

Reina arose dazed and battered. She couldn't see anything so she reached for her phone and tried to turn on her flashlight, but cut her fingers in the process. She dropped her phone in pain realizing that her screen was shattered and her phone wrecked.

She heard Tiffany calling out her name so she yelled back, "Tiff

I'm down here somewhere! Help me please it's cold and I can't see anything!"

Tiffany could hear her echoes but could not pinpoint where they were coming from. She was shaking in terror, panicking because Reina was hurt and alone and she couldn't tell from which direction she had fallen. When she illuminated the ground she saw several steep paths of stairs leading down into what looked like crypts.

Reina continued yelling out for help until she heard a hiss. Something was in the lower passageway with her! She became paralyzed in fear as she heard the sound of something slithering on the ground getting closer! Then she heard some weeping, like a woman! *Was it Tiffany?! It didn't sound like Tiffany!* It didn't sound like anyone or thing that she had heard before! It got closer, and closer, almost a whisper by her side and then stopped. Then she heard some heavy footsteps and a woman's low moan, as if in pain or suffering.

Reina was about to have a heart attack! This thing or woman was right up on her! Her fight or flight adrenalin kicked in, but before she mustered the courage to flee in the dark two cold hands reached out form the dark and grabbed her!

She still couldn't see, but sensed that a very heavy and naked woman jumped on top of her, pinning her to the ground. This unknown monster started to feel very much like a woman as it squeezed her legs around Reina's waist and continued to pin her arms to her sides.

Reina was finally able to give off a panicked scream, but it was quickly silenced and muffled by a long, wet tongue. The creature's mouth sealed around Reina's lips and slithered it's long tongue deep into Reina's throat and even down into her stomach! It began to vomit a warm slimy liquid down her throat!

She shook in terror as the creature continued to squeeze Reina deep into its feminine body while pumping this liquid down her throat. Reina's head was bobbing back in forth as more slime went down.  Her belly was filling up with it.  She slowly began to lose conscious as she heard Tiffany still screaming for her somewhere in the dark.  Tears flowed down Reina's eyes and then she finally blacked out.

# CHAPTER 10 –
# BREAK TIME

Meanwhile, at the far end of the ruins and away from everyone else, Charlie and Desiree were exploring another tunnel when they caught the scent of a very sweet nectar or perhaps some herbs. As they got closer, Desiree spotted a large amount of flowering vines that appeared to be growing down into a large room from a crack in the wall. Desiree walked up close and inhaled their fragrance. Their smell was very sweet indeed.

Next to the flowers were ancient drawings carved into the wall. It looked like two female figures and a man. One female was sleeping with the man and the other was off in the distance, alone, and surrounded with what looked like a halo.

"These are the drawings of Xkeban and Utz Colel!" proclaimed Charlie. "See that's Xkeban being promiscuous with a man and way over there is Utz with her shiny halo full of purity!"

Desiree looked at Charlie again in amazement, he was on his game today! "Charlie did you sleep in a Holiday Inn Last Night or something? You sure do know a lot,"

Charlie decided to take a picture of the artwork as well as the nice smelling flowers. Then picked a handful of them and put them into his backpack to show the group later on.

"You know Charlie, we are by ourselves right now and I don't hear anyone else from our party." Desiree had walked over to the light shining down from the crack in the wall, right next to the sweet smelling flowers. Her red hair looked so soft and inviting. She was looking at Charlie with envy. She wanted him now.

Charlie got the hint and went in for a kiss. Desiree was more than ready for it. She French kissed him again, but this time she wasn't floating in the water in the Bahamas. She was on level ground without the need to tread water. Both Charlie and Desiree became lost within their feelings as she continued to thoroughly invade his mouth and throat with her tongue.

Desiree became even more and more infatuated with Charlie, she then grasped the back of his ass and pulled him into her waiting hips. Charlie's head disappeared into her cleavage and his dick immediately came to attention. Desiree felt it and used her massive body weight to bring Charlie to the ground.

"You're all mine now Charlie!" and with that Desiree furiously began to unbuckle his belt and strip off his clothes. She then stripped and they were both naked on the cold floor. The cold floor was startling at first, but then Desiree's thick warm body flowed over Charlie as climbed on top of him with her full naked body weight. He moaned and rolled his eyes back as Desiree began to slowly rub her naked body up and down his. She surround his head within her boobs and rubbed them all over his face and as she did Charlie latched on and began sucking on them.

Desiree spread her hips wide and rubbed her hot wet pussy deep into his groin. His dick got harder and harder to the point when she knew it was time and then she reached down and held his penis up and into position. She slowly lowered herself back down onto Charlie and as soon as the tip of his penis felt her pussy lips, a loud shriek erupted in the background!

"Holy Shit!" shrieked Desiree as she leaped off Charlie. They both stared at each other and affirmed they both heard what sounded like Reina. Quickly they got dressed and started running back out of the room.

Then Charlie stopped and said, "Wait I forgot something!" "WTF Charlie let's go!" "Just one minute", he ran back a short distance and found his bag on the floor with his phone light. He picked it up and then both Desiree and him high tailed it back to base camp.

# CHAPTER 11 – RESCUE PARTY

Both Lauren and Ray seemed to be walking in circles when they suddenly heard the scream and they recognized it was Reina's.

They both made their way running to the location and then they heard Tiffany yelling out for Reina as well. Ray and Lauren got closer and yelled out to Tiffany. She heard them and they slowly caught up with each other. Tiffany was hysterical and crying loudly.

"I lost Reina, I think she fell down somewhere, she was yelling out for help but then stopped!"

Lauren and Ray tried to comfort her and as they did all three used their phone lights to search the various dark rooms. Periodically they called out for Desiree and Charlie but they were too far away. Ray then remembered that everyone's phones were indeed cell phones and not just flashlights! He sent out a group text explaining that he and Lauren found Tiffany and that they were searching for Reina. That Reina was hurt and lost, but they were going to find her.

Both Charlie and Desiree were finally near the ruin entrance when they got the group text, the cell signals were getting really bad. They responded back that they were going to wait at the base camp with John and Brian. Reina didn't respond to the group text and neither did Brian or John.

When Desiree and Charlie finally made it to base camp John and Brian were no where to be found. Charlie then group-texted and asked where both John and Brian had gone. They didn't answer.

"WTF?!" yelled Charlie.  Both Lauren and Ray then got a text back from Charlie that the other guys seemed to have left them.  Ray tried calling to clarify, but the phone signals were so weak that he couldn't get a ring tone.  He, Lauren, and Tiffany then continued searching for Reina.  After about fifteen more agonizing minutes Lauren spotted what looked like a few slimy footprints leading out from a dark hallway.

They followed the hallway for several minutes and heard what sounded like shivering, moaning.  They ran closer and closer to the sound, finding more and more slimy footsteps until suddenly Lauren's phone light spotted Reina on the floor shaking horribly, probably in shock.

Reina's eyes caught the phone light and quickly faced them. Her eyes were full of terror and rage and she was holding her belly as she violently twisted her body on the floor.  Then she vomited up some slimy substance and finally screamed one last time.  She collapsed back down onto the floor unconscious.

Brian saw the latest group text going back and forth from Ray and Charlie.  He hadn't made it that far and began to feel guilty for abandoning them like John did.  He thought about the new pack of girls he met up with and then felt a surge to continue onto the ship, but then he remembered how much Reina seemed to adore him.

He knew that he had hurt her feelings and now to find out that she was injured and needed help was too much for him to bear. He turned back around and jogged back to base camp with the sun nearly setting.  While on his way back, he called John who actually picked up his phone this time.

"Hey John, it sounds like Reina is hurt bad.  I'm going back man.  I don't really like her but I can't leave her out there.  I need to help get her back to the ship."

John understood Brian and told him, "Yo man you just do you okay.  All of them fools got lost and hurt themselves, I ain't trying to waste my spring break with them, but you do you man." John then hung up the phone. He looked out to the dropping sunset on the beach and breathed the fresh air. *I just got out of that damned jungle and I'm sure as shit not going back for nobody.*

Back at base camp Lauren, Charlie, and Desiree were all arguing about what do next. The sun had just set and it was dark out. None of them had any camping supplies, food, or water. Reina was clearly hurt by something and Tiffany was still mentally in shambles.

Ray was adamant that they press through the dark in the Jungle, despite the fact that they could barely see through the brush with a full moon overhead. Lauren was trying to explain that even with the best of intentions they might end up injuring Reina more in the process or even one of themselves because the brush was so thick. They needed to stay the night, perhaps at the entrance to the ruins and wait for daylight again before heading back.

Unfortunately, everyone's cell phone's batteries were nearly empty at that point and their signal reception was completely useless. Charlie was beginning to side with Lauren on staying, but then asked if going back into the Ruins was wise based on Reina's attack.

As the three continued to argue Tiffany walked over to Reina who was sitting down with her back leaning against the giant Ceiba tree and staring back at the ruins. "Hey baby, I'm so sorry we got separated, please are you okay? Can you at least speak to me?"

Reina still didn't answer and Tiffany began to tear up. Then Reina seemed to try and clear her throat and say something back, but was having trouble so Tiffany got closer to her. Reina tried to whisper something but Tiffany couldn't hear what she said so Tiffany sat down right next to Reina and asked, "What is it?"

Reina looked at tiffany eye to eye as if thinking deeply of something, but unwilling to speak it. Quick as a snake she grabbed Tiffany with both her arms and brought her to the ground and with the same motion she sealed her mouth around Tiffany's and pressed down on her with her full body weight.

Somehow this five foot nothing Latina had the strength of ten men and was now French kissing Tiffany on the ground while the others continued to argue oblivious to what was happening behind them.

Tiffany felt Reina's unusually long warm tongue slither it's way down her throat, nearly choking her, and it seemed to be forcing some slimy liquid down her throat! Reina kept this up for probably a few minutes as Tiffany began to go into shock. Finally, Reina withdrew her tongue and got off Tiffany. She stared down and silently watched as Tiffany was laying on the ground shaking and holding her stomach in pain.

Reina then silently walked away into the forest, discarding her outer clothes and leaving on just a white one-piece undergarment in the process.

Ray, Charlie, and Lauren finally stopped arguing and came to a decision that it was safer to just wait until the morning with the daylight. They turned around and walked back to Tiffany and Reina. Both of them were gone and there was more of that strange slimy fluid on the ground!

"Oh shit!" said Ray. Everyone then began to panic yelling out for both Tiffany and Reina.

"We need to split up and find them" said Lauren. To which both Ray and Charlie absolutely refused. It seemed that splitting up is what got them into this situation in the first place. They began to argue again.

# CHAPTER 12 – LOVERS REUNITED

Brian was getting closer to the base camp when he recognized the voices of Ray and Lauren off in the distance arguing with each other. Then he heard Charlie as well. His anxiety began to reside. He was a nervous wreck ever since he decided to walk back to base camp. Half because he was worried what the group would say to him and half because he had been alone in the jungle hearing all kinds of crazy noises.

As he got closer to the group her heard some twigs break nearby and spun around. Something else was nearby. He kept shining his light into the direction of the noise and was getting ready to yell out to the group when he saw what looked like a girl slowly walking towards him.

He shined the light in her face and instantly recognized that it was Reina. She didn't seem scared or frightened. She was walking just fine as well, almost too fine he thought. Her hips gently swayed from side to side, rather seductively and she ran her hand through her long and wild sexy black hair.

She walked closer to Brian and now he saw her better through some moonlight shining from above the tree tops. She was wearing a skimpy white gown that reflected the moonlight. Reina was smiling and her eyes, seemingly more black then brown and they were staring directly at him.

Her breasts gently swayed from side to side as she got closer and then she whispered out his name, "Brian".

He collapsed to his knees and began to sob to Reina as she walked closer.  He had betrayed her and yet through all of this she still seemed to have feelings for him.  As he sobbed Reina closed the full distance and stopped but a few inches from him.  Then he heard her take off her white gown and toss it aside.

He looked up at her as she kneeled down onto the ground and drew his head and face into her naked bosom.  She then rubbed his back with one hand and began to passionately kiss Brian.  She licked away all of his salty tears and swallowed them down.  Then she began kissing Brian down his neck. Perhaps this was her way of saying, "I forgive you."

He hit the ground with a thud as Reina pushed him down and proceeded to strip off his clothes.  Something had changed in Reina.  This did not seem to be her at all why didn't she at least explain what happened or why she was out here all alone.  *How does this small girl have the strength to take him down the way she just did?*

Soon he forgot all about his questions as she spread her hips open and mounted him.  She leaned over Brian and began giving him slimy tongue baths all over his body.  Brian felt his stress melt away and closed his eyes as Reina's tongue covered every square inch of him.

Then she turned around and began to sixty-nine Brian on the jungle floor. Her hot mouth and plump lips worked him good.  He was in heaven, staring at her thick ass surrounding his face while she deep throated him over and over.  It didn't take long for him to completely blow his load down her throat, and when he did Reina clamped her lips all the way down to the base of his shaft and began sucking and swallowing it all down into her belly.

Brian kept cuming and going into spasms as Reina continued to gulp it all down. *This is beyond heaven! This Latina chick knows how to deep throat, she ain't even stopping or coming up for air! Wait a second, how is she still going and why has she not stopped to breath?*

Then he felt Reina squeeze her legs and thighs stronger around his body as well as her arms.  She had him wrapped and pinned to the ground with immense strength as she continued to milk his dick dry.

Brian soon realized that there were no more sounds coming from the forest, he couldn't even hear the friends in the background arguing anymore, but the deep gulping sounds of Reina's mouth. It was as if he and Reina had become isolated in the Jungle.

He began to feel weak, almost unable to move and Reina finally took one deep swallow with the suction of a Dyson vacuum and gulped the last of his cum down. He must have been cuming continuously for minutes! *How as that even possible?!*

Reina slowly got up of the ground and faced him. He tried to get up as well but couldn't. *Shit I can't move!* Then he tried to talk but his mouth couldn't make any words. He looked up at Reina who seemed to have a wicked smile as she rubbed her belly and breasts.

She seemed to be getting bigger...no, he was shrinking! He watched in horror as he shrank all the way down to the size of a small mouse and now Reina and the rest of the forest was huge! She was a giantess to him!

Reina carefully picked Brian off the ground and slowly rubbed him into her belly like a damp cloth. He heard a deep growl, like her stomach was getting ready to eat! He looked up again and her mouth was wide open dripping saliva down in giant globs!

Reina brought Brian all the way up to her face and licked her lips. She raised him high above her open mouth with his legs hanging down, unable to move. He look down to see Reina undulating her throat muscles and moving her tongue around.

She began to lower him down into her mouth. The warm moist air greeted his feet and he began to sob, still unable to speak or scream for help. Reina slowly closed her lips around him. She wrapped her long tongue around his torso and slowly began sucking Brian the rest of the way into her mouth. Hi slast vision was of the jungle tree line and the moonlight. He saw the cavernous mouth begin to cut out his vision from the sides and soon he was watching her lips close in front of him.

Reina tongued Brian relentlessly inside her wet mouth coating his whole body with her saliva. Then she leaned her head back and swallowed him whole with a satisfying moan. Reina resumed her slow walk out of the forest and towards the coast.

After some time Brian regained the ability to move his limbs again and he felt his mouth loosen. He struggles furiously to escape as Reina's warm mucus-coated stomach walls were mashing him up and massaging his whole body. He seemed to have grown back a little in size, but only to the confines of the space in Reina's stomach.

Reina felt the strange movements in her stomach for the first time and looked. Her belly looked pregnant. She stared in wonder as she watched what looked like a face and then and some hand prints moving along the walls of her belly, trying to press out. It tickled and felt good to her.

Reina also heard what appears to be some weird muffled voice crying out her name from within her belly. She giggled and laughed at it. She didn't even really understand any of it in that it just felt so damn good like a shot of pure dopamine crack-cocaine.

Deep inside Reina's stomach, Brian had started fade out to the sounds of her heartbeat. Bubbly digestion enzymes were pouring in from the stomach lining and getting louder. He felt his skin begin to tingle as the flesh coffin of Reina's belly simultaneously began to squeeze in on him from all sides. He closed his eyes and whispered out one last time, "Reina please." There was no response.

After hours of walking, Reina finally arrived at the edge of the forest overlooking the coast. She saw the lights of the cruise ship against the silhouette of the city. She looked down at her pregnant belly and gently caressed it with her hands. She couldn't feel anymore struggles, no more muffled cries.

Then like a snake, her abdominals began to constrict and roll her belly around like a belly dancer. She could feel the large mass inside of her coming apart with mushy, slurping sounds. Her belly movements, combined with her stomach muscles and digestive enzymes were mashing Brian's remains down into a soupy mush. Reina felt a surge of pleasure run throughout her whole body as his form liquefied within her.

She sat down in the sand, right next to the breaking waves and moved one hand into her pussy and the other one onto one of her breasts. Reina started to finger herself and build up an orgasm as her round belly began to shrink. Brian's liquefied remains were being sucked into her intestines.

As her belly got smaller and smaller Reina speed up her masturbation violently against the crashing waves until she climaxed hard. A warm river of cum flowed out of her pussy, down the wet sand and into the ocean.

Looking back down at her belly, she saw that her once pregnant hump was all but slush  She still had a big belly, but it wasn't massively pregnant, like earlier. Reina felt a strange sensation in both her breasts and her ass. It felt like they were slowly growing in size. Her body's quick work of Brian made her drowsy with food coma. She walked back up the beach a bit and then laid down in the sand staring up at the stars to let her body finish processing him while she slept.

As Reina closed her eyes, she heard the sounds of male screaming nearby. The sounds were more of joy then terror. She walks closer to the sound and saw two figures, one massive black woman bent over on the beach and a tall white man thrusting his hips into her rear.

# CHAPTER 13 – IT'S MY DUTY TO PLEASE THAT BOOTY!

John was in the fuck of his lifetime. He was thrusting his dick hard and fast inside Tiffany's anus. It was wet, hot and slimy as fuck! Her giant pea-shaped ass was literally swallowing up his hips with each thrust!

He was up standing tall so he could see her entire body jiggle as he fucked it. It felt so amazing inside of her tight anus! He legs started to tire since he had just walked out of the jungle so he got down onto his knees and kept going.

Tiffany began to emit a low moaning sound as John fucked away. His dick was already fully erect, but he wanted to feel as much of her tight sphincter as possible before he pulled out.

Almost out nowhere, a fully naked Reina appeared from the side slowly walking up to both him and Tiffany.

"WTF are you doing out here? What happened to your clothes" yelled John.

No answer.

"Are you all right Reina?" still no answer. She kept walking towards them.

Earlier in the evening, John was staring at the ship from the outskirts of the jungle when he saw Tiffany. He was surprised as hell. He thought that she was back in the Ruins with the group tending to Reina or at least that is what the group text conveyed.

He had called out to her as she walked to him but she did not answer. She only smiled back and she was naked. Quickly he typed in-group text that he spotted Tiffany on the beach! He didn't take a picture, he just dropped his phone and stared at her in awe. Her dreadlocks were completely undone and her long black hair was trialing down her back. In the full moon, John watched as the silhouette of her massive body walked closer. Her breasts were huge almost twice the size of his head! Then there was that massive thick ass, swaying from side to side, calling his name.

Tiffany stopped just short of him and turned around. She got down on her hands and knees and the propped up her giant pear ass into the air facing John. Her hips began to sway from side to side. Tiffany was twerking! That was all John needed to see before he quickly took off his clothes and jammed his thick rod right into her waiting ass hole.

Now John was staring at a very peculiar Reina right in front of both Tiffany and himself.

Tiffany looked up off the ground at Reina with a big smile, which Reina returned.

*WTF is going on? Ain't this some kinky shit!* He also noticed that Reina seemed to be a little bigger than usual. Her ass and boobs were much larger and plumper than he had noticed before.

He watched Reina crawl up to Tiffany and press one of her boobs right into Tiffany's face.

John almost busted right there as he watched Tiffany suck on Reina's boobs. She wasn't just sucking, she was drinking! She was swallowing up Reina's breast milk while John was deep inside Tiffany's ass hole. Reina then smiled a seductive grin back at John. It was too much and John completely exploded inside Tiffany's anus, deep into her rectum. In response, Tiffany's anal sphincter clamped down hard on John's dick making him spew even more.

He looked back up at Reina as both she and Tiffany seemed to be moaning in ecstasy. Still, he couldn't pull out against her tight anus as it seemed to be sucking his dick up in tight. Reina got up and walked behind John. John watched her thick Latina breasts and curvaceous body jiggle as she moved.

When she got behind John she wrapped her arms around him and leaned up against his back. Then she used her body to push John deeper into Tiffany's ass.

Tiffany leaned back heavy into John. Now John was being squashed between the two.

He climaxed a again and looked up to see Reina's open mouth descending to his face. She began to French kiss John while Tiffany continued to grind and ass clap her thick ass into John's hips.

Eventually her anus released his dick and John fell back to the beach absolutely wiped out. He looked up at both Reina and Tiffany. Tiffany was still clapping her ass and twerking for John.

He continued to watch, mesmerized like a moth to a flame. Her ass was getting larger and larger, and so did the trees in the background!

*Oh shit he was shit I'm shrinking!* He tried to move but found that he was unable to. He looked back up at Reina, now a towering giant with her face barely visible beyond her massive boobs. Then Tiffany stopped ass clapping and spread her ass cheeks wide open. She winked her anus several times in front of him.

John was about the size of her anus if not a little smaller and her colossal peach ass cheeks surrounded him on both sides. Reina then grabbed his small feet and carefully began feeding them into Tiffany's anus!

John looked back and forth at Reina who had a wicked smile and then back at the giant ass ring that she was pushing him into. He tried to yell but couldn't speak. Reina pushed him into his waist and then removed her hand. She just sat there watching John and giggled.

Tiffany began to moan and then slowly wiggles her ass from side to side. She continued to Hold her ass cheeks open for Reina to watch.  Slowly Tiffany's ass began to suck John further into her rectum instead of pushing him out.  He looked back in desperation at Reina who was now fingering her pussy and bucking her hips.

The warm, slimy rectum continued to suck John inside.  The smell was strong with a combination of both sweat and a slimy filth at the outer ring of her anus.  He eventually got sucked in all the way and as the anus sphincter closed behind his head with a loud slurp!  As this happened he heard Reina scream in orgasm.

John was having a shitty day.

Tiffany's rectum slowly sucked John deeper inside her bowels, now into her colon and large intestine.  John felt like toothpaste getting squeezed down a very long slimy tube.  He felt the slimy intestinal lining tightly pulse and move him deeper into Tiffany. *How am I still alive?  How am I still breathing?  Is this fucking for real!*  Tiffany was still twerking and ass clapping as she felt the lump of John travel slowly through her intensities on its way to her stomach.

John eventually regained the ability to move and speak again, but it was too late.  He was on a one-way trip deep inside Tiffany's monster ass.  His body also tried to grow back but there was no space to grow as his confines got tighter and tighter.  John's skin began to burn and he slowly began to fade out of consciousness as his body traveled through her never-ending flesh tunnel.

When John's body finally arrived in Tiffany's gut, he was almost mush from the enzymes that coated him inside her intestines. Reina and Tiffany had been making out all night at this point. Reina felt up Tiffany's mushy belly licking and rubbing her warm spit all over it.  Then Reina went down on Tiffany and proceeded to eat her out.  Tiffany moaned in ecstasy as Reina's warm, long tongue thoroughly invaded her pussy.

Tiffany looked down to see that her own boobs were still growing a little.  Eventually her belly shrank down enough that she could see Reina's face hard at work pleasing her.  Tiffany climaxed all over Reina's face and Reina slurped and swallowed it all up.  They then both curled up on the beach and listened to the crashing waves.  They both feel into a deep sleep as their bodies continued to absorb the remains of Brian and John.

# CHAPTER 14 - REGROUPING

When the morning broke Charlie, Desiree, and Lauren had finally made it back onboard the cruise ship. They were tired, scared, nut mostly worn down. All of their phones had completely drained batteries since they took turns using them as flashlights to get out of the jungle.

Desperate to know what happened to the rest of their friends they each went back into their cabins and plugged in their cellphones to charge. After several agonizing minutes, they began to receive group text messages.

"John – Oh fuck guys I think I just spotted Tiffany, I thought she was with all of you. Where are you guys?"

"Brian – Guys I think I spotted Reina!" Then there was a picture of her that Brian took with his phone.

It was Reina all right with long dark hair and black hair. Her eyes seemed dark, but warm along with her smile. Charlie seemed to recall something he saw while researching the Mayan ruins the other day but it left his mind before the idea could hold once he saw the next text pop up.

"John – I'm sorry you guys are having such a bad time. I had to leave. I was just making things worse. Maybe I'll see you all back on the ship."

"Brian – Hey, that sounds horrible! I'm on my way back."

Charlie, Lauren, Ray, and Desiree took turns trying to text them back, but there was no response. Then they tried to text Reina and Tiffany. Again no response. The ship was getting ready to leave port and they all panicked because they couldn't spot missing friends or a least hear anything from them.

They met back up at a lounge and then went to a customer service center to ask about their friends. One of the employees heard their conversation and mentioned that there were two naked women found unconscious on the beach by some fellow spring breakers.

"One was a rather large African American and the other was possible Hispanic. A medical team brought them in after they were found by some fellow passengers. We thought they were drunk because both of them were apparently trying to make out with the girls who spotted them on the beach. Heard it was really sloppy if you know my meaning! Anyways those girls that found them left after our medical team arrived, so that's how we figured they didn't know each other. We couldn't detect any alcohol or drugs on them, but their bodies were farting up a storm when we brough them down to the infirmary!"

Ray interjected, "What what?! Was there anything else unusual about them?"

The employee continued, "They passed out again after we brought them into the ship and they have been asleep ever since we received them. Let's bring you all down so you can see that they are safe." Then the employee escorted them down.

Once they arrived, the group could see that the medical staff had dressed both Tiffany and Reina with some type of medical gowns.

"Are you friends or family?" said the lead nurse. "No, well yes we are actually friends from this trip, see" Lauren showed him a recent Facebook page with a picture of all of them from the snorkeling trip.

"Well Ma'am we think they may be suffering from some type of constipation. They must have eaten a lot and passed out. Their bellies were pretty big with food when they arrived, but they have been shrinking down for the past several hours and they are releasing a lot of gas. The girls have even been burping in their sleep!"

"WTF?!" From almost everyone in the group.

"We really think we need to pump out the contents of their stomachs in case they ate something toxic while ashore, but we don't have any of that kind of gear here. I have already scheduled an emergency medivac flight to the US. It's currently scheduled to arrive this evening. Once they get here we will transport them on the flight and send them on their way. We need one of you as their friends to sign a patient consent form for the service,"

Ray silently signed the consents to surgery forms, his hands shaking all over the place. "Don't worry we will take care of them" the nurse said.

The whole group was devastated. None of them had any words of encouragement or anything to say in general, they all just looked at each other and sobbed. They left Tiffany & Reina to the care of the ship and began to walk away.

Ray stopped and asked the nurse, "Hey where there any guys on the beach with them?" He pointed to Laurens's FB picture on the phone.

None of the staff recognized Brian or John and there were no men in general that had checked into the infirmary for the entire trip.

The ship was sailing into the evening and what was left of their group met up for dinner. Ray spoke up. "Maybe Brian and John are off happily fucking away their stress and don't want to bother with us anymore".

It did seem logical. After all, both of them had texted that night in the ruins that they had seen the missing girls and Brian had even taken a picture of Reina. It was no secret that both of them were trying to hook back up with the girls they had pissed off.

"Maybe they slipped the girls roofies and tried to take advantage of them, but dumped them and ran away when they saw they were pregnant!" blurted Desiree.

"We don't know that, but yes it's possible," said Lauren. "But the nurses couldn't detect any drugs in their system." Lauren was trying to think if either Brian or John were capable of drugging girls on the trip. She didn't sense any hostility from them, but it was well known that some guys were known to drug women and take advantage of them at parties. It was always a risk.

"This all started when we entered those damn ruins! I should have never taken you all there!" cried Lauren. "That slime we found on Reina, something did this to her and it might have affected Tiffany as well!"

Everyone went silent again. Charlie pondered a little during the silence, *was it possible that what ever happened to Reina in the ruins was a part of all this? If so, WTF was it?!*

They finished their meals and decided that their remaining group would meet up in the ship's next port of Cozumel tomorrow. No more risky adventures. They were just going to relax all day at Playa Mia.

As they got up to separate, Lauren held onto Ray's hands and Desiree onto Charlie's. Both the guys realized that the girls did not want to sleep alone. The couples then went to bed together that night. No funny business, just warm cuddling and kisses to calm the nerves.

When Desiree was fast, asleep Charlie got up filled a glass cup with water and some of the sweet-smelling flours he picked back at the ruins. He placed it in her bathroom, next to her large hot tub. Next, he pulled out the gift spa package with some wine, a champagne glass, and some bottled water and a sealed envelope with her name on it. Charlie desperately wanted to tell Desiree how he felt about her. He hoped that his gifts would help.

He walked back out of the bathroom and stared at Desiree sleeping in her bed. He loved her long shiny red hair. He watched her chest move up and down as she breathed. Her body was so thick and plump, it always felt good when he was with her. Desiree and him had gotten to know each other on the trip. *Should I start asking about her family tomorrow or is that to soon?* He thought.

She made him feel at home, she was his sanctuary, his oasis. *If and when I get laid by this woman it's going to be epic.* He then walked out of stateroom and softly closed the door behind him. He put her spare room key in his pocket and walked back to his own cabin.

Both couples had given each other their spare room keys that night. Ray also left Lauren's room and went back to his own cabin, but along the way he spotted what looked like a few wild girls all over some guy in the hallway. They were having sex with him or possibly, raping him in the hallway? Well if was the other way around Ray probably would have done something, but instead he thought, *That lucky MF* and closed his door to let the spring breakers do their thing.

# CHAPTER 15 - RELAXING IN COZUMEL

That morning the friends got together on the launch deck and took a small ferry into Cozumel. As they loaded into a departing ferry Lauren swapped spots with Ray so Charlie was flanked by both the girls.

Charlie blushed and Ray began to laugh. With a little tease Lauren then whispered to Charlie, "Hey their stranger, you know you're kinda cute" then she winked at Desiree who then winked back at Lauren and they both looked at Charlie seductively.

They both broke out laughing. Lauren was messing with him, but not Desiree. Her one hand was on his thigh as she pressed her hips and chests closer in on Charlie.

"Thanks for the note, Charlie, and yes you are all mine" she said. She kissed his cheek and brought him in for a hug. Charlie's head settled nicely in between her soft boobs as she went down and kissed his face.

Lauren and Ray then hugged each other, glad to see that things were working out.

It had been several hours on the white beach sands of Playa Mia. Everyone was tanning and just trying to recover from the night at the ruins. Their legs were sore from getting lost in the jungle and eventually breaking out to find the coast.

Lauren and Desiree got up at some point to go the lady's restroom and Ray was working on getting lunch for everyone.

Charlie was left behind and was watching a group of spring breakers playing volleyball on the beach. They were having the time of their lives and so was he! Even with his friends group cut in half Charlie still had plenty of company with just the other three. Desiree was now a close friend on his Facebook page and she even gave him the address to her college dorm. He already had her phone number. *What could possibly be any better than this right now?*

Far off in the distance, next to the volleyball match Charlie saw an odd woman just staring into the crowds. She had long dark hair and was wearing a very skimpy thong. She slowly walked onto the beach and closer to the match, then she turned and was facing Charlie's direction. She began to walk again, this time straight for Charlie. He lifted up his shades and sat up in his chair. Something was oddly strange about this girl. Her bust was huge and her thick ass was jiggling as she walked, but her face and composure looked like she was in a trance of some sort.

She paused again and smiled. Ray interrupted Charlie and asked for help in getting the food. As the two went back to pickup the food order Charlie told Ray that he though he saw someone like Reina at the park, but that she was much bigger and acting kind of strange. Charlie said she had long dark hair and was Hispanic or Mexican. Ray laughed and said, "You will probably see a lot of long black hair sexy Latinas on this trip Charlie."

The group finished their meals and hit up some water slides and jet skis. They then got back on a returning ferry before sunset so they could eat dinner on the ship and watch the sunset form the comfort of the pool deck. They all shared a hot tub and looked out at the sunset. They sat back and relaxed while it got dark.

Without warning, several young girls walked into their hot tub unannounced. Apparently, they felt cold and had stomach aches so the hot tub was their answer. Just past the closet pool to their hot tub the friends saw more horny spring breakers getting hot and heavy. They watched as some guys and girls hooked up and then went back to supposedly a stateroom to "finish the deal" behind closed doors. As they retired for the evening, the friends could hear a few couples that seemed to be missing their partners. It was typical for people to be lost and drunk on these cruises. *Just hope they don't fall overboard*, Charlie thought.

As Charlie tried to go to bed for the evening, he heard spring breakers fucking around the ship. There were moans of pleasure and shaking walls followed by orgasmic screams and then silence. He thought to himself, *why didn't I just go sleep with Desiree tonight?* Hell, if everyone was banging, he should have joined in. He wondered if Ray and Lauren were part of that group or if that had tried to go to sleep like he was.

# CHAPTER 16 – THE NIGHT SHIFT

Back in the ship's infirmary, Larry was keeping watch. The medivac flight got postponed to the following day due to bad weather. He began his scheduled bedside check and walked in-between both Tiffany and Reina to check on their vitals. He looked at his notes and then stared at their bellies, back and forth.

His shift notes mentioned that they were constipated and were awaiting a medivac flight to go state side to pump out their stomachs. He looked back at their bellies and didn't see any signs of constipation. They looked completely normal, maybe a little chubby, but completely normal.

If anything, both of their breasts were very large and it seemed their butts were nice and thick too. He started to write in his notepad when a hand grabbed him! It was Reina's and she was sitting up!

His face was pale from freight, but he regained his composure and asked, "Ma'am it's good to see you are finally awa...THUD"

Larry turned around. Tiffany had gotten up out of her bed and was now standing directly behind him. She had taken off her clothes and her giant black breasts were level with his faces, only inches away.

Then he heard Reina get completely out of bed. He turned around to see her remove her clothes as well.

He dropped his notepad in shock.

Tiffany and Reina simultaneously proceeded to strip Larry of his clothes. They quickly sandwiched his naked body between the two of them and proceeded to lick and kiss Larry all over his body. His dick started to become erect. Tiffany pulled him in close and buried him between her massive boobs while Reina went to work licking his ass cheeks with her long slimy tongue.

Tiffany's warm body enveloped Larry within the cold infirmary. It felt good. It felt overwhelming. It felt safe. She was rubbing his shoulders and eventually started to move her hands further down to his lower back. Then she grabbed the sides of Larry's ass cheeks and gently pulled them apart.

Reina shoved her face right into Larry's exposed ass crack and gave him a slow and sensual rim job. Larry's dick instantly hardened all the way with Tiffany watching. She squatted down and completely swallowed his dick all the way back into her throat. Then Reina thrust her very long tongue deep into his rectum. Larry moaned and began to shake with intense pleasure.

The phone started to ring but Larry remained bound between his two patients, getting more and more excited. He was nearing ejaculation. Tiffany shoved her mouth and lips right onto the base of his groin, sending his rigid penis all the way down her warm throat. It squeezed him hard and the suction was intense. At the same time, Reina wiggled her tongue vigorously around the inside of Larry's asshole, deep into his rectum. He came multiple times and Tiffany swallowed it all down with loud gulps.

Several minutes later loud slurping and gulping sounds echoed from inside the infirmary. Both Reina and Tiffany calmly re-dressed and walked out. Tiffany's giant belly jiggled up and down as Larry was screaming and fighting for all his life. Once outside the infirmary the two spilt up and went their separate ways.

Lauren called the infirmary several times to find out if Tiffany and Reina made their medivac flight, but nobody was picking up. *Doesn't the ship's infirmary have a night watch in place?* She left a voicemail and made a note to call back the next day.

She spent the rest of her evening sorting through her research notes.  One of her pages was a depiction of the ancient Mayan seductress, Xtabay.  She read more into the description and saw pictures of a long dark, haired woman with black eyes wearing a white gown.  Xtabay was described as an evil Mayan spirit that seduced men and consumed them after sex.

Lauren looked up into the air and pondered something.  Then she pulled out her phone and looked at the image that Brian had sent via group text.  She looked back and forth at her research and the picture and gasped.  She dropped the phone and nearly fainted.  Lauren collected herself, calmed her nerves with some vodka and then pulled out a second phone in her drawer.  She texted a message back to her research partner in the states with a simple message, "IT'S REAL!  HELP US!"

Tiffany had just walked out of a lady's restroom and was proceeding down below decks towards the engineering spaces.  She had dumbed the very last remains of John out of her colon and into the ship's septic system.  This made more room in her intestines to accept Larry once her stomach broke him down.  The additional heat from the nearby machinery kept her whole body nice and warm.  This accelerated her metabolism and eventually Larry stopped struggling.  She fell asleep on the floor as her giant belly slowly began to shrink, breaking down Larry into mush and sending his remains into her waiting intestines.

Reina kept walking until she heard the sounds of some loud techno dance music and people cheering in the background.  She slowly walked up to the dance club and saw it was full of young people, both girls and guys.  She smiled and walked into the club.  She kissed every single girl on the dance floor, even the ones by the bar.  Some of them tried to resist at first but quickly found themselves swallowing thick slimy mucus from Reina.

None of the guys watching intervened.  They actually began to cheer thinking that they were all caught in the middle of a lesbian orgy.  Minutes later all of the girls dropped to the floor and started convulsing.  It was Ladies Night so the guys were outnumbered by about three to one.  It was a massacre.

Only a few guys made it out of the club.  The ones slowly digesting away inside a girl's belly as she mindlessly wandered back to her cabin.  The rest of the guys were experiencing various phases of forced sex or being swallowed alive.  Some guys had a single woman on top of them grinding away, on the verge of making them climax.  Others were being smothered and ganged fucked by multiple women.

The ones who had already ejaculated inside of a girl watched in horror as their bodies shrank and were then inserted into one of the women's various orifices.  None of the men would ever be seen again.

Eventually all of the late night parties throughout the ship stopped.  Scores of women where all returning to their cabins to sleep off their meals or find another fresh female to convert.

Reina disappeared into the ship, hunting and full of lust.

# CHAPTER 17 – BEYOND TABOO

Jim was on his seventh Corona, possibly more. The bartender shut him off at some point and left. "Fucking bitch!" Another swig, then "Fuck you all bitch ass mother fuckers! Ain't nobody fucking work hard like me and you just take my mother fucking money!" His eyes slightly full of rage but mostly drunk. He looked over at his audience at the bar ...empty bar stools. Then he looked back at his corona and chucked it. "Fuck this shit".

He started to guzzle the bottles of oxygen water the bartender left him when he noticed two rather voluptuous women approaching from the side of the pool deck. One had a big slice of cake with thick cream or icing on the top and the other had a martini or something. Both of them looked fine as hell in their clubbing clothes no doubt. That is probably where they came from. They sat down next to him a few stools away. He watched them as the one woman began to slowly eat her cake, but somehow dropped a few pieces with the icing right down her cleavage. The other woman came over and began to lick it off and swallow it down. Jim almost chocked on his drink.

They both looked over at him and licked their lips. Jim was so transfixed that he forgot to answer his vibrating cell phone. The women stood up and began walking over to him. *Oh shit,* He thought.

Jim stood up, leaving his cellphone on the bar table and slowly backed away. Part of him wanted to see where this was going, his dick now pointing straight out under his swim trunks. He looked down at his hand with his wedding ring and looked back up at the advancing women.

"Hey what you gals up to?" No answer.

"Is there something I can help you with?" Still no answer.

Both of them were walking faster and smiling at him. Jim panicked and started walking backwards, but then fell right into the pool. He splashed around for a bit in the cool water and looked up out of the pool. The two women had stopped advancing and were just staring at him.

"Fuck it. I'll just swim a little till these bitches leave."

He managed to swim a few laps and then he heard a splash by the shallow end. He immediately stopped and treaded water looking at the splash. Nothing. He looked back up at where the two women were and it was just one now, still staring at him.

Then a rather petite young girl, possibly a college freshman stood up from under the water and was staring at Jim in the pool. Almost immediately thought he recognized her but kept on swimming away.

She started to breaststroke toward Jim. *What is happening? Does this girl know me?* He swam back to the edge of the pool in a shallow spot where his head was above the water and watched her approach. It looked like it was his older daughter that was away in college or so he thought, but there weren't any tattoos on her skin and her hair was half died with blue highlights.

She had glittery lips and dark blue shadow above her eyes that was slowly coming off in the water. The girl continued to swim at him and eventually she was right in front of him.

"Amy is that you? Amy?!"

He swore it must have been his daughter, but now that she was closer, he saw that her breasts seemed to be a little bigger than before and all of her skin imperfections were gone.

"This can't be I didn't think you were..." *KISS*.

Amy closed the rest of the distance, embraced her father and began kissing him. Jim pushed her off.

"No Amy, stop!"

She came back, more aggressive now and rubbed her large boobs and body deep into him.  He began to get excited and terrified at the same time.  She was Soo much stronger than him and now his own daughter was making out with him in the pool, forcibly.  He knew that she was a spoiled brat.  This was not her typical behavior.  She hated Jim!

*Splash*!  This time a large splash came from behind him and the woman that was watching Jim at the bar had jumped into the pool behind him and was now restraining Jim close to her own body.  She was strong as well!

He watched as his daughters head slowly went under water and then he felt her drag his swim trunks down.  Amy swallowed up his exposed dick underwater as the other woman wrapped Jim up in her arms.  She was licking Jim's neck and nibbling his ears while his daughter sucked away.  Jim heard his cellphone vibrate again on the bar table.  His wife must still be trying to track him down after their last argument.

*Imagine the surprise if Lisa walks out and finds her daughter soul sucking me.* Amy's suction got stronger as she had been down there for minutes without coming up for air and Jim couldn't free himself from the woman behind him.

He thought his daughter was in trouble since she had not come up for air, possibly for several minutes.  Yet she was still sucking him.  The woman behind Jim was now licking his entire face with her sticky tug, her wet hair down and covering Jim's head from sight.  She pushed Jim further into her plump body as Jim's daughter sucked harder.

Jim climaxed and felt his cum flow down his daughter's throat.  She swallowed it down, still underwater through all of this.  He became dizzy and it seemed his world was getting bigger.  The woman's breasts behind him started to feel enormous.

He felt a warm tunnel of flesh swallow his feet, and began sucking him down and crept up to his legs, his thighs. He looked around in terror and saw that the pool deck was enormous! The woman behind him let go and he saw that she was giant as well. Somehow he had shrunken!

His heart was racing as recognized the giant face of his daughter directly under the water. She had him in her mouth! Slowly she rose up above the water with Jim captive in her lips. He looked down at her massive body and felt her lips part. He began to slide down.

He couldn't yell or move. He looked one last time at the bar top with his cellphone and saw the other giant woman now fingering herself. His daughter then tilted her head back and swallowed her father down into her belly.


Lisa finally arrived at the pool deck, furious. "Why doesn't he ever answer his damn phone when he drinks?"

She knew Jim was out here, it was his usual venting place for the evenings. She called him again and then heard a vibrating phone nearby. She walked over and saw his phone vibrating on the bar top table. *That figures.*

As she walked closer, she heard a moan and some splashing by one of the hot tubs. *That asshole is probably fucking with some girl right now!*

Lisa walked over to the hot tub and to her surprise, she saw her daughter Amy, apparently pregnant and sitting in the hot tub.

"Amy?! What are doing here I thought you were away in college!"

Amy just smiles back.

"Hello Earth to Amy! Oh, shit and are you pregnant? WTF Amy! Why didn't you tell me and want is going on!"

As she stares at her daughter's belly she swears that she can see a baby kicking and moving around.

"Amy get the fuck out of there! You should be in a hot tub if you are pregnant! For fuck sake Amy say something!"

There was another noise behind Lisa and she turned around to see another woman come up and embrace her. She kissed Lisa directly in the mouth and slithered a long, slimy tongue down her throat.

Lisa tried to scream but only emitted a few gargled sounds as the woman took her to the ground. Lisa looked over to see her daughter masturbating in the hot tub and rubbing her pregnant belly. Lisa slowly lost consciousness and began to shake.

Minutes later, both Lisa and the other woman are in the hot tub sucking away on Amy's breasts. The increased sexual stimuli and warm temperature of the hot tub were speeding up Amy's digestive system. Her father felt the slippery stomach walls close in on him like a killer sleeping bag.

He cried out his daughter's name, "Amy!" one last time.

It barely resonated as a muffled sound from within her belly against the loud hot tub.

Jim's body slowly compressed into mush and he blacked out just as Amy climaxed, pouring her fresh cum into the warm water. She leaned back and closed her eyes in sexual bliss as her mother and the other woman continued to sucking milk from her breasts.

# CHAPTER 18 - ONE FINAL PORT VISIT

The friends were on the last port visit of the trip in George Town, Grand Cayman.  The girls and guys decided to split up and do the shopping and site seeing separately.  Ray was with Charlie and Lauren was with Desiree.

The guys were spending all day talking about the whole trip, the fun snorkeling meet up, the dance club, the crazy Mayan ruins, Cozumel, and the girls.  They hit up some more bars and talked about hanging out with their girlfriends after the break.

Lauren and Desiree actually wanted to get as pretty as they could for the evening.  This was going to be the special night with their boyfriends.  They had booked all-day spa therapy sessions in town and each searched for a killer dress to wear that evening.

As Ray and Charlie walked around town they seemed to notice something a little off.

"Hey man didn't we like always see that girl over there with her man like all through the cruise at the pool deck?" said Ray.

"Yeah, they were always together, now that I think of it I don't think we have seen that dude all day."

More and more Charles & Ray started to realize that this port visit was full of mostly women.  *Where were all the guys at?  Was there some sports bet or game on back at the ship?  Maybe they weren't interested in shopping.*

Charlie spotted a woman sitting at a table with a big pregnant belly.  She was rubbing it with her hands, her head lying back in her chair, seemingly relaxed, possibly humming something. Charlie and Ray noticed more and more pregnant women that they swear did not look pregnant at the beginning of the cruise. It wasn't just that. The women that were not pregnant seemed exceptionally voluptuous to the point that their curvy assets were almost busting out of the seams of their clothes!

As they continued to walk up the market they spotted more of these "big" women just staring blankly at nothing. Some would turn their heads and stare at the two of them as they walked by. Some were even…touching themselves when the guys walked by. Their facial expressions were that of pure lust. It was actually getting late and they hadn't heard back from either Lauren or Desiree so they tried calling and texting, but the girls did not answer.

Something wasn't right. Charlie felt the exact same feeling that he had back in Cozumel when that one Latina girl stared at him. Now many of the women around them seemed to exhibit the same behavior. It was getting darker outside and still no answer from the girls.

Charlie and Ray were desperately searching all the shops and spas but could not find them and with each visit, they were attracting more and more girl's attention. Then Charlie had a quick panic attack as he remembered what he had forgotten the day earlier. The picture text that Brian had sent the group of Reina on the night of the ruins reminded Charlie of the Mayan mythology he read earlier in the week.

He told Ray to look at the photo and they both stared at Reina's picture. Then Charlie opened up another tab on his screen and compared it to wiki page talking about an ancient evil woman called Xtabay that hunted down men at night. She would seduce them, have sex with them, and then consume their bodies and souls for eternity.

Ray then remembered what Lauren was researching on that day they all ate brunch together before going to the ruins.

"Doesn't she look like Xtabay, Reina I mean?" said Charles. "Yeah man she kinda does" They had stopped walking in the middle of the market while comparing wiki pictures against Reina's photo while the woman around them stared to close in.

They looked up and saw that they were not just being watched, but stalked!

"Ray we need to get the hell out of here and back to the boat, we need to read up on Lauren's research material now!"

Ray agreed and said they could get in her cabin with the spare room key she gave him. The girls were supposed to meet up with them back on the ship anyway for dinner. Maybe they would catch them there.

As Charles and Ray made their way to the port, they spotted more and more pregnant women either lounging in a chair or laying down on the beach as they rubbed their squirming bellies. Some of them were actually masturbating and seemed like a few of them were grinding into each other heavily and making out like lesbian lovers.

The they both heard an orgasmic scream nearby and saw one of them that appeared to be flexing and rolling her belly and hips as her giant pregnant belly started to collapse in size. She then leaned back and pressed down on her now mushy belly as it slowly broke down the contents. She climaxed and sprayed the whole beach around her with warm cum as her belly deflated.

*Shit did her boobs just get a little bigger just now?*

She then turned and looked over at Charlie and Ray, licked her lips and emitted a large wet burp! They broke out to a run and high tailed into to the ship!

# CHAPTER 19 – SHIT HAS HIT THE FAN

By the time they got onboard the sun was minutes away from setting. Both of them flew past what seemed like hundreds of spring breakers making out and having sex all throughout the ship. More pregnant bellies and more big voluptuous women stalking them as they ran by.

Finally, they got to Lauren's room (she was not there) and eagerly read her research notes. They soon discovered that Lauren was actually a history major. She was a cover agent charged with finding the lost remains of the Mayan temple not to just gather artifacts, but to try to recover a sample of a giant snake that had been haunting the jungles of Costa Maya for centuries.

They opened up a dark-covered envelope that had money and passports for quick departure from Mexico once she got the sample. Next to the research paper was a clear jar with some hardened slime on the inside.

They heard a maid knock on Lauren's neighbor's cabin door.

"Room Service".

They heard the door open and listened to some confused guy saying that he didn't order room service for that evening. It went silent so Charlie and Ray pressed their ears to the wall. They heard the maid kissing the neighbor loudly. Next, they heard a gentle thud on some box springs. *The mattress!* The maid fucking the life out of the guy, thrusting herself down on top of him relentlessly.

Minutes later hey heard him climax and then there was nothing.

They both pressed their ears closer to the cabin wall and heard some loud gulping sounds and possibly some very faint muffles or screams. Then they heard some more female moaning that led up to an orgasmic scream just like on the beach! Their eyes widened it terror. Whatever this was it was on the ship!

With their ears still pressed close to the wall, they heard the maid get up, get dressed, and walk out of the neighbor's stateroom. Ray and Charlie carefully opened the door in time to see the maid turn and leave the hallway, but as she turned, they saw that she had a large pregnant belly, that was squirming! They then walked into the neighbors open cabin to discover the guys clothes and items strewn on the floor. There was a massive load of fresh cum all over the sheets! It was dripping down the sides of the bed and onto the floor!

They quickly went back into Lauren's room and continued reading her research. Supposedly the other ancient Mayan lover, Xkeban, was the equal and opposite match to Xtabay before she died, and when she died her grave was covered with sweet smelling flowers. The flowers looked exactly like the ones Charlie picked with Desiree.

"That's it!" Charlie exclaimed. "Those flowers I picked back in the ruins are supposed to be the equal opposite likeness of this Xtabay that we might have released. Maybe if I can get the girls to smell the flowers it will knock them out of whatever it is that is happening to them!"

They both ran back towards Charlie's cabin, but saw that the entire hallway was filled with voracious girls. The girls spotted them and began to chase. Charlie and Ray had to go back up to the pool deck as a detour. When they got to the top, what they saw was an orgasmic battle beyond belief.

There were girls fucking guys whichever way to Sunday. Guys fucking girls, and as the guys would climax, became weak and began to shrink! Charlie and Ray watched in horror as the girls they had sex with either swallowed them whole, shoved them into their vaginas or took turns helping to push the other girl's man into their thick asses!

There were girls screaming, apparently non-converted yet that were fighting to keep the other girls from kissing them with their slimy mouths. As soon as some of the guys noticed what was really happening, they tried to erect a barrier of lounge gear near the pool and defend themselves from the girls. It didn't work. Soon they were all stripped naked on the ground and getting ridden by the unnaturally strong women. Some ejaculated immediately, others were able to hold out for longer, but they all climaxed eventually.

Charlie kept looking around and spotted his neighbor. It was the older man he saw masturbating on his cabin balcony earlier in the week to the beachgoers in the Bahamas. Now the old man was stripped naked and being held down by half a dozen horny girls. Somehow, he had not climaxed and was not shrinking, *perhaps he has ED*, Charlie thought.

More girls arrived, seemingly determined to devour him so they teamed up and simultaneously began kissing and licking his body all over. He was covered in girls, buried underneath them as the loud slurping and sucking sounds continued. Some were rubbing their privates on him and into his face. It was working. Charlie and Ray watched the old man's dick finally get some circulation and became rigid.

Then one of the bigger girls moved into position and began cowboy riding the old man into heaven. He came after maybe a minute or so and the riding girl slowly stopped. The rest of the girls then resumed licking and sucking him all over as his body began to shrink. His disappeared in that crowd of wiggling flesh, into the belly of one of the girls, swallowed whole.

"Run Charlie!" Yelled Ray.

As they darted past more girls and into the hallway, a few gave chase. They caught up to them and pinned the guys down the ground. Both Charlie and Ray flailed around like mad, undid their clothes and escaped naked with the girls holding onto their garments.

Charlie looked back into the distance and watched the few remaining guys get taken. Suddenly a thick Mexican maid walked out of a side room in front of them and bear-hugged Ray. She took him to the floor and immediately mounted him.

Charlie ran back but Ray screamed at him to leave him. More girls started filling into the hallways and Charlie left Ray as the big Mexican easily pinned his arms to his sides, wrapped up his legs with her thighs and slid her warm pussy on top of Ray's stallion. She leaned back and began to ride Ray, her hips grinding down hard into him.

Charlie had to leave Ray. He ran fast down the remainder of the hall and finally got to his room. He closed the door and collapsed on his bed crying out tears. All of his friends that he met on this trip were now gone some way or another. It became clear to Charlie that Reina probably devoured Brian and Tiffany got to John. Of the original wolf club members it was down to just Ray and Charlie, and Ray was probably going to be digesting deep inside the belly of thick Mexican maid after she got him to climax.

It was only a matter of time. All the girls, lost to some man-devouring curse of an ancient Mayan ruin that they should never have visited! Then Charlie remembered the flowers. He quickly opened up his back pack, but his heart sank as soon as he saw them. They had all lost their sent and shriveled up because he left them in his bag for several days. They probably were not going to work. Lost in thought he stared at the shriveled flowers for minutes. *They might still work* he thought. Then he heard his door open up behind him. The only other person with his room key was...Desiree.

Ray was probably the strongest man on the ship, but this maid was insanely strong. She easily held him to the ground as she proceeded to dominate him. At first, she still had on the top half of her servicing uniform and he watched in awe as her massive boobs wiggled and bumped another while she rode him.

He focused on her name tag and saw MIA written on it. Then he looked up at that sexy Mexican face rising up and down. He saw her jade earrings swaying and reflecting some of the ship's lighting. His eyes widened, then he noticed the gold bracelet on her one arm pinning his to his side. It was the old maid Mia fucking the shit out of him!

He looked back at her face and could easily see that with maybe some more wrinkles and skin imperfections...somehow it was her! He gasped, partially from one of her deep thrusts, but also from the realization that his maid was fucking him. Then she stopped.

While Ray was still staring back dumbfounded, she removed her top servicing uniform and bra and threw them to the side. She undid her hair bun and let it all hang down. Her super fine smooth caramel skin was glistening with pearly beads of sweet. Her massive breasts were now gently resting on her chest as they rose up and down with her breathing. She giggled and then firmly placed her arms back at his side. *Fuck Ray! That was your chance to escape!* he thought. Then she continued riding him. The other girls who had been watching then left to go find meals of their own.

Ray thought about how some porn star guys could control their erections, hold out on video shoots, and cum on demand. *Hell, if they can do it so can I!* Her pace quickened along with her breathing. The maid started to alternate between smothering Ray with her large boobs while rocking him and then leaning back and deep grinding her hips and ass into his pelvis. It was beginning to work.

She sensed this and then put more effort into grinding her thick ass into him, arousing Ray even more. She looked down at Ray's face to see his reaction, his mouth was open, breathing quick gasps of air. Ray was about cum and the maid knew it. Her vaginal muscles tightened up and his hips began to spasm! He felt his cum traveling up the penile shaft to the head and watched in slow motion as the maid smiled at him.

She leaned her head back and began to gasp on the verge of climax, pussy muscles tightening even more, her large breasts flopping in the air. Ray closed his eyes and began to moan. It was over for him.

Suddenly Lauren came out of nowhere and knocked the maid off of Ray!

Ray's burst open like a cum fountain into the air just as the maid's pussy was clear of his cock. Lauren then ripped off some of her clothing and wiped up the cum off of Ray and lit the cum-soaked rag on fire with a lighter. The maid got back up and chased after them.

"Ray there is something I need to tell you!" yelled Lauren. Neither of them was in any condition to sit down and chat, but Lauren felt that she needed to come clean in about her story.

"Where the fuck is Desiree! What is happening Lauren!" Ray yelled back.

"Ray, we got separated! Desiree...she...sh...SMASH"

An extremely pregnant looking woman had just walked out of a side room, directly into Lauren's path. Lauren couldn't stop her forward momentum and ran into her. Ray ran back to try and get the woman off of Lauren, but she said, "It's okay, once they have swallowed a victim whole, they lose all aggression until the victim is completely absorbed, sort of like a predator that has just eaten."

Sure, as shit the woman got up and just kept walking on her way with no care in the world about either of them. They noticed the man inside her belly was still struggling for all of his worth.

"He'll probably be completely digested by tomorrow and that's when she will be dangerous again." Lauren was way to calm and knowledgeable about what was happening.

They found an open ship storeroom with nobody in it, closed the door and Lauren laid out the details.

"Once a woman is infected or converted she will continuously try and seduce a male victim and during the act of sex, her body strength and adrenaline spike. She uses this power to constrain him and pleasures him to ejaculation. If the guy resists approach or the infected woman is ravenous enough, she will flat out attempt to pin him and force him into sex. Then once the male ejaculates inside of her he will begin to shrink and lose the ability to move or talk."

Ray heard all of this and still could not understand it all.

"But how!" yelled Ray.

"Ray, we don't know and this should not be scientifically possible, but the victims are eventually swallowed up one way or another and at that point they will slowly grow back to the confines of whatever cavity they are in. The infected woman's digestive system or reproductive system eventually breaks down the man into mush and absorbs him into her body. This makes the infected woman more voluptuous and ravenous. We term them Voracious".

"Lauren WTF?! And what do you mean by whatever way and whatever cavity?!"

"Ray, please try and understand I'm still learning as well. But what I saw, I can only imagine the horror those men felt."

Ray paced around quickly, clearly upset about all of this.

"Well why doesn't the world know about this and who the fuck is this WE?!"

Lauren then looked down onto the ground and said, "Ray, I can't tell you that, at least not now, but I swear to you I never thought it would happen at this scale."

This truly was very disturbing, but Lauren didn't answer how all this shit got started in the first place or why it seemed that only women were getting infected and only men were on the menu.

"So how did this begin and why is it spreading amongst the

women?”

Lauren took a swig of some vodka in the store and continued her explanation.

“We believe the source origin is somewhere near or in those ancient Mayan ruins at Costa Maya. It all started with reports of some village men disappearing and sittings of either a very large snake or a very beautiful woman deep in the jungle. I was sent in to do some investigative research near those ruins to see if I could find anything. It seemed like a joke Ray! Nobody at the agency took it as a real threat, just some ancient fable and probably some dumb ass village men being killed in the jungle. I swear Ray I had no idea it would be like this. I thought it was a vacation gig! You all seemed like a fun adventuring group and there were no realized threats…said from the jungle creatures themselves.”

She paused and started to cry, “I don’t know how to stop it! I don’t know what to do Ray!”

Ray held her hand and calmly spoke, “If the legend you researched is true, I think that Charlie may have found something that could reverse whatever it is that is happening to these women. He brought it back with him from the ruins and it’s in his cabin”

Lauren’s eyes widened up with hope, so they agreed to go to Charlie’s cabin to see what they could do.

The hallway was empty again and Lauren and Ray made a dash for it, but the same maid who was chasing them earlier emerged from a hidden spot and lunged at Ray.

Lauren blocked her attempt and they continued to run, but not before the maid spit a huge wad of slime directly into Lauren’s face! She quickly wiped it away and resumed evasion. The maid then stopped pursing them and went in another direction.

“Shit Lauren that was close!” said Ray. He didn’t see the maid spit onto Lauren. He then spotted a large gym, the one that he had worked out with John a few days ago. They might be able to craft some weapons form the gear there. Lauren just hoped that none of it got in her mouth

They ran into the gym and locked the door from the inside. Lauren seemed to be dizzy form all the running. She walked into the middle of the gym and collapsed. At first, she told Ray that she just needed to rest but then she began to convulse and spasm violently.

"No Lauren no! Please no!" Ray cried. He looked back at the entrance to the gym they had just run into and saw an army of girls blocking their path. It was hopeless now. He watched Lauren eventually stop shaking. She got up and took off her clothes. Ray watched Lauren approach him in slow motion, there was no way out and he knew that tying to fight her now would just increase the amount of pain both mentally and physically. He then took of his own clothes off and laid down on the ground.

Lauren walked up to him and looked down at Ray with a look of intense desire. She turned around and began to squat her thighs directly over his face. Then she spread her hips open and face-sat Ray deep into her wet pussy. Ray remembered this from the wrestling fight back in the Bahamas. He welcomed it. This time there wasn't a thin layer of honey-soaked panties in between his face and her cunt.

At least he was going to die by the one he loved and not some stranger. No sooner had Ray's face disappeared into her neither's did Lauren's mouth slowly engulf and swallow Ray's entire dick. He may have ejaculated a huge load right before the maid almost got him, but Lauren seemed to know how to excite Ray again. She kept shoving his face into her pussy and deep throating his shaft. He loved the scent of her pussy all over his face and began to eat her out in return.

She responded to this stimulus by sucking harder and longer. In fact, she wasn't coming up for air at all. The suction was constant and continuous. Ray felt his cum traveling up his shaft and to his penis head again, but this time he didn't fight it. Ray climaxed down Lauren's throat and she eagerly gulped it all down.

Lauren kept Ray pinned to the floor with her hot wet pussy seemingly getting bigger and swallowing up his whole head. He knew what was happening. Eventually Lauren stopped sucking and then squatted down more as her pussy continued to slurp up Ray.

His shrunken legs and feet were still hanging out of Lauren when she orgasmed and came all over the gym floor. The orgasm was so intense that it echoed all over the gym. Lauren's hips were shaking wildly with pleasure, she was breathing very hard and fast. Still her strong vagina didn't release Ray with the orgasm. She resumed slurping Ray up past her vagina into her cervix. He sensed his feet disappear from the cold gym air and into her warm vagina. His head squeezed through into her womb. His chest and the rest of his body soon followed. To Ray, Lauren's womb was a peaceful and inviting place There weren't any painful, scorching acids. Instead, he felt his body glide into a warm fleshy tube, gently pulsing around him.

Lauren, got down and mounted a nearby foam roller noodle with her hips. She began to pillow hump the foam roller and moan. Ray heard the moans from inside and felt the womb around him begin to compress all over his body. Her heartbeat was very rapid and the vibrations enhanced the feeling of the warm flesh surrounding him. She continued to pick up speed and more of his body disappeared into the compressing flesh. Finally, he heard Lauren scream out his name, "Ray!"

She climaxed hard and her womb completely mashed Ray into a liquid pulp all at once. Lauren gushed out hot cum onto the gym floor through the orgasm and collapsed onto the floor. She then fell asleep as her uterus went to work absorbing Ray's mushy remains.

# CHAPTER 20 –
# RED RED WINE

Charlie spun around to see Desiree standing in his open doorway. Her eyes had a dark color to their iris and they were looking directly at him. Her stomach began to growl and she licked her lips. Desiree was turned indeed. She had used her spare key to enter his room!

Quickly Charlie reached into his bag of dead flowers and threw them into her direction. She just smiled, walked in and then closed his cabin door behind her. *Shit!* The flowers had no effect. Desiree was wearing a very sexy red outfit showcasing her entire cleavage. It wrapped tightly around her sexy belly. Her long red hair was smooth as silk and running down either side of her shoulders. Desiree silently took of her whole gown and panties and threw them to the side. *If there ever was a way to go I chose this.* Charlie thought.

Desiree climbed up onto the bed and slowly crawled towards Charlie. Her massive boobs were hanging down with her long red hair. She rubbed her body onto him, as she inched closer to his face. Her warm skin was soft and smooth, her hair a little tickly. As she continued to rub her body over him, Charlie's dick began to stiffen up.

*Oh no, please not so soon, let me enjoy this* he thought. Then her hips finally slid up to his groin and her pussy was already wet and waiting for him. Desiree was right up on Charlie's face now. She opened her mouth and French kissed him. This time her tongue was extremely long and it went all the way down his throat. At the same time, she began to rub her open pussy up and down his dick.

*Take me*, he thought.

The ship's loudspeakers came to life and started playing, UB40's Red Red Wine song. It seems that a crewmember was trying to drown out the sounds of chaos with a gentle Caribbean tune. *How thoughtful, this is definitely the way to go!* Charlie's dick began to stiffen.

Desiree removed her tongue from his throat and looked at him confused. *Did the dead flowers actually work?* he thought. Maybe it was enough to interrupt her trance. This was he chance! He quickly freed his arms and hands from his sides and tried to push her off him, but his hands simply sank into her massive boobs and she didn't budge one bit.

Desiree continued crawling up towards his face. His opportunity was over just like that. She grabbed the back of his head and shoved Charlie face first directly into breast flesh heaven. She used her other hand to position his stiff dick up into position and slowly inserted him into her warm pussy. She was absolutely wet as fuck! Desiree paused again and now with both arms she pulled Charlie tighter into her boobs and started to hump and slow grind on top of him. Desiree was massive! Charlie's whole body was completely underneath her and partially buried within it. He was indeed completely hers now as she ravished him over and over.

After several more minutes Charlie felt his pre-cum breaking through and whispered, "Desiree, I love you" and with that he completely erupted inside of her pussy. Charlie's toes curled up and his eyes rolled back into his head with a long gasp of pleasure.

Desiree grabbed Charlies' back and pulled his head deep in-between her breasts. She leaned back with her thick ass and milked his cum away while she gyrated her hips side to side. Charlie felt himself get weak and begin to shrink as Desiree held him tight and continued to bear hug him while burying him into her warm body.

He continued to shrink. Soon his head was partially buried into her belly and wrapped up within her boobs. He could hear her stomach growling in anticipation of its meal…, which was Charlie. Finally, he shrunk down to the size of her hand and he looked up to see her massive breasts on either side of him with her big belly in front of him.

Desiree picked him up and lifted Charlie to her smiling face. She stuck out her tongue and slowly licked his whole body with sticky, warm saliva. Unable to speak or scream Charlie just smiled tearfully as Desiree opened her mouth and lifted him up into the air. He looked down to see his final vision of the woman he fell in love with for the trip.

Her hot breath bellowed up from bellow onto his feet and he shuddered in anticipation of what was next. Charlie felt her giant tongue slide up to meet him and her lips slowly closed around his waist.

Desiree held him there halfway out of her mouth and explored his little naked body with her giant tongue. It shot up out from her lips and glided up and down his body coating him with even more warm saliva. Then she slowly sucked him down into her mouth with just his head above her lips.

She moaned and sucked him all the way inside her mouth, tossing him around with her tongue with more saliva, getting him into position to swallow. Charlie felt his legs beginning to enter her throat and then Desiree walked up to the mirror and opened her mouth.

Charlie cleared his eyes of the thick saliva and looked back out from the opening of her mouth when he sensed the fresh air. It seemed she was staring at him in the mirror! She kept him in limbo for several minutes as he continued to watch her. Desiree just kept staring at him and rubbing her belly. Her throat would occasionally begin to suck him down, but then quickly push him back up. *Was she fighting the urge to swallow him? Maybe the dried flowers were starting to work?*

Warm humid air continued to flow up from her stomach and the saliva in her mouth maintained a thick coating all over his body. Just as Charlie felt the ability to wiggle, his fingers and toes, she brought up one hand and slowly waved goodbye to him in the mirror. *Shit, I think she recognized me!*

Suddenly Charlie felt the muscles in his own mouth loosen up just as he freed one hand to wave back and he quickly yelled out, "Desiree I Love y..." Gulp, Gulp, Gulp.

Before he could finish his words, Desiree swallowed him down into her hot rumbling gut and continued to massage her belly. Once her throat muscles squeezed Charlie through her esophagus he landed into a warm pile of mush. From the smell it he guessed it was a cheese croissant. He felt that some of it had melted completely and was being sucked into some fleshy sphincter nearby.

"Oh shit the small intestine!" He screamed in horror and tried to get himself out of the sinking mush. Then her stomach walls collapsed the empty space around him as Desiree's massive hands began to caress and rub her belly from the outside!

He could hear Desiree moaning in joy as she explored her belly. He wasn't even fully digested and he knew the small intestine would be a super long and slow death if he hadn't suffocated yet or been squeezed into mush like her lunch. She continued to rub her belly. Charlie slipped and fell back into the mush like quicksand. He heard the sphincter open up again and draw in more of the digested food down into the small intestines.

To his surprise, his body slowly began to grow back and he was no longer in danger of being sucked down into her intestines... yet. His body stopped growing as soon as it filled up the remaining space in her stomach. Now Charlie was curled up into a tight ball while Desiree's thick muscular stomach tightly began to massage his body all over.

More slippery fluids began to seep out of the walls in his flesh prison and made his skin tingle. He could hear and feel her heartbeat, her breathing. It was a full body massage squeezing and marinating him in more of her juices. He tried pushing back against her thick walls for minutes, sometimes pushing is face into the flesh to see if Desiree saw his impression from the outside of her belly. *Just like the other poor guys he had seen swallowed up earlier.* Now he knew what they had gone through, what he was going through. He truly belonged to Desiree now, figuratively and literally.

*Maybe one day she'll look down at her body and think of me. Then again, she'll probably never know what happened. Nobody will ever see me again.* Charlie pondered more about his life, the things he had done and not done. He thought of his family, work, and friends. He remembered how much fun he experienced on this spring break cruise and all of the new friends he made.

Ray, the cool guy who started it all and brought Charlie into his wolf pack with John and Brian. The first time he Saw Desiree at the snorkeling trip and how she kissed him in the ocean. Sitting next to her at dinner and later getting deep throated at the bar while Tiffany held him tight. Oh yeah Tiff, she was huge. Reina, then Lauren. The memories flowed through his head, as the remaining air thinned out. Lastly, he recalled Desiree on top of him in his cabin, full of lust. She completely rocked his world and took away his virginity in the process. Now she was absorbing him into her body.

With the last of his energy, he pressed his face and hands into the slimy mucus walls and screamed out, "Desiree, please! Please! Nooooooo!" He sank back into the mush and closed his eyes. It was hopeless.

Charlie listened to the sounds of digestion getting louder all around him. He felt his skin tingling even more. He began to envision Desiree's warm inviting face smiling at him as they both held onto each other in the water, back in the Bahamas. He remembered that day so well. She was coming in for a slow French kiss with a friendly smile. Her skin was so smooth and soft in the water. Charlie kept playing the lyrics of the Red Red Wine song in his head as looped that memory over and over. The smooth stomach walls gently engulfed Charlie like a warm water bed, his body disappearing into its folds while the warm enzymes rubbed all over his skin.  The feeling was divine.  He was inside his sanctuary, his oasis.  Desiree was his red wine.  Charlie ejaculated one last time and blacked out.

# CHAPTER 21 - THIS IS THE END

The ship's crew found out too late that some terrible contagion was effecting the passengers. Most of them were below deck and in the engineering departments as the killer orgies erupted topside and throughout the ship. A few of them managed to get the ship underway and set the navigation to autopilot. Its destination was set to return to Fort Lauderdale, Florida.

The captain of the boat had locked himself into his stateroom and was trying to call out for help. The ship's cell service and satellite communications were mysteriously not working. He couldn't reach anyone and the bridge was completely overrun.

He scanned through all of the security cameras. All of his crew-members were either gone or "being taken". He managed to spot a few of the female crew walking around with large squirming bellies. In despair, he looked out of his porthole window for any signs of help.

Off in the distance he saw a mid-sized, unmarked yacht following his ship out of port. It had launched a small drone and it was flying in their direction. He slapped his cabin wall hard and celebrated for like one second and then he heard an electronic beep followed by the sound of his door opening behind him. He slowly turned around to see two of his female crew hands in the room facing him. One of them was holding a ship's master electronic room key. It was his Entertainment Director, somehow she appeared to have regressed back into a younger age and was showcasing a very curvy figure. As soon as she made eye contact with the Captain, she began to unzip her uniform.  Both her and the other female crewmember continued walking to him.

The unidentified drone operators had never seen anything like this before.  All throughout the decks, guys were disappearing at an alarming rate.  At first, the women would slowly advance to seduce their prey, but when most of the ship was converted they became very aggressive and actively chased the men down.  It didn't matter if the men weren't interested.  Once a guy was overtaken he would soon be stripped of his clothes and pinned to a surface with overwhelming strength.

A woman would force extreme sexual pleasure on a man, sometimes by multiple women.  Then he would climax and shrink down in size.  The operators couldn't understand why the men couldn't fight back or why they were shrinking.  Then again, they really couldn't understand any of it besides the fact that all of the women were exceptionally attractive and voluptuous.

Most of the women with squirming bellies were going topside and laying down on the pool deck.  Some appeared to still have their room keys.  Those that did went back into the ship.  A few close-up flights confirmed that women were going back into their cabins and adjusting their air conditioning.

All of the hot tubs were completely packed.  The heat appeared to accelerate the rate of digestion.  The drone operators than concluded that the women in their cabins were also increasing the temperatures in their rooms.  Infected women without male prey helped to pleasure the women actively digesting one. This also appeared to speed up digestion.

"Any word from our agent?"

"No Sir, her last message to us was…IT'S REAL! HELP US!"

"Contact Langley, send in the air assets"

Desiree silently entered her cabin and closed the door behind her.  She was caressing her giant gut and slowly began rolling and pulsing her belly.  She felt the warm enzymes now washing over her meal as it smooshed up against her stomach walls. Desiree was still horny as ever and felt the need for more stimulation. She looked over to her bed with a lustful gaze and climbed on top.

She got onto her bed, grabbed a large fluffy pillow, and crammed it against her pussy. Then she began to slow-hump it. She tilted her head back and closed her eyes, focusing on the soft fabric rubbing into her clitoris. She speed up the motion and ground down harder on the pillow. The pleasure was overtaking her. Soon her whole bed was rocking hard back and forth. She was moaning in ecstasy.

Desiree looked down at her large belly flopping up and down with her boobs, her slick red hair now wild and flying all over the place. Desiree felt herself stating to cum and her hips began to spasm. Then something caught her attention.

She stopped grinding on the pillow just short of climaxing and looked down at her belly. *Why is my stomach so big? Where am I?* Desiree started to become more aware of her surroundings. She looked around and began to sniff. She caught a sweet scent. She got up out of her bed and walked to the bathroom.

There on the countertop she noticed a couple of white flowers next to the sink. It was in a glass vase of water. She walked right over and sniffed them. They smelled so good and each time she would sniff some more. Desiree's memories began to come back to her.

She was studying to become a nurse. She had recently gone on a cruise...possibly this one. Snorkeling with some girls and then... some guys. That's right, she was on spring break. She looked back over at the flowers and saw an open envelope with her name on, a bottle of rose red wine, champagne glass, and a spa kit with face cleansers and a bath bomb! *The staff really went all out this time!* She thought. She soon remembered that this was her second cruise and she was familiar with finding chocolates or folded towels on her bed. Some cruise lines did this to help spread happiness to their customers by giving them a little surprise in their freshly serviced cabin.

Desiree removed her gown and set it aside. She turned on the water to her luxury hot tub and began unpacking the spa kit. She placed the bath bomb into the warm water and turned on the water jets along with the bubbling air nozzles.

The envelope was probably another thank you letter or maybe a voucher for something. *I'll get to that later, drinks first.* She opened up the wine and filled up her glass. She got into the extra-large tub and sank down into the water. The warm swirling water, foamy suds, rose fragrance, and sweet smell from the flowers in the bathroom made her completely relax.

Desiree soon realized that she had drank nearly the whole bottle of wine so she picked up the oxygenated water from the spa kit and guzzled it all down. *Don't want to get dehydrated in a hot tub,* she thought. Then she leaned her head back and closed her eyes. She began to daydream about her trip and slowly more memories came back.

She remembered Charlie. A smile came to her face as she started to envision him and all of the earlier activities of the week. She drank some of the oxygenated water from the spa kit it had a nice fruity flavor to it as well and would help wave off any headaches form the wine.

She slipped on hand under the suds and began fingering her pussy. Her mind drifted to the memory of the club as she went down on Charlie, probably for his first time. She began to pick up the pace with her fingers and then used her other hand to feel up her large boobs and thick belly.

In her mind, Desiree saw a cloud of dead flowers hit her face and then fall down to the floor. Then she sees Charlie on a bed directly in front of her and he is all alone. She recalls herself going into a lustful surge, taking off her clothes and then getting on top of Charlie. Back in the hot tub, Desiree is nearing orgasm. Her dream continues as if she is riding Charlie for hours. Finally, she looks down at Charlie's face as she thrusts her hips hard and deep. She feels his warm virgin cum fill her completely.

She watches his eyes go back into his head as he shudders underneath her massive body. She wraps him up with a big hug, shoving his head in-between her large boobs, and continues riding him away while her thick ass cheeks grind down into his pelvis. She climaxes hard inside the hot tub and relaxes in bliss.

Then a strange vision floated into her mind. Desiree is now staring at herself in the mirror why she does not know. Her eyes have a dark black shade to them and she begins to smile wickedly into the mirror while rubbing her thick belly.

She slowly opens up her mouth wide and see's Charlie halfway down her throat! Desiree raises one hand and slowly waves goodbye back to him in the mirror.

At this point, she is thrashing hard in the tub and trying to wake up.

Then she sees what looks like Charlie trying to wave back with one hand and possibly shouting something before he sinks down her throat. His outline traveling down her neck, in-between her large boobs and slowly fading away as it approaches her belly.

She licks her lip and continue to rub her belly. It seems to grow a little and jiggle. Then to her horror, she sees what looks like the impression of Charlie's hands and face pushing against her stomach from within. She can hear his muffled screams! He is screaming her name!

Desiree is on verge of waking up and she is crying out Charlie's name in the bathtub.

Back in her dream, Charlie's impressions then sink back inside, disappearing from her skin's surface as she continues rubbing her belly. Desiree smiles again in to the mirror and begins to moan in pleasure. She emits a loud wet burp and giggles back into the mirror as her stomach starts to shrink back down.

Instantly Desiree opened her eyes and stands up out of the hot tub! Her heartbeat was racing and she began to have a panic attack.

She teared the note from the open the envelope and read it.

*Dear Desiree,*

*I know we have only known each other for a short time, but you are the love of my life. No, I am not some silly drunk trying to score. Well maybe I am trying to score because you are hot, but I really love you and hope you feel the same way about me too.*

*Love,*

*Charlie*

*PS. – I'm all yours ;)*

Desiree's memory instantly flashed back! She stood up and spun around her room. She spotted her cellphone and tried to text Charlie. No answer. Then she tried to call, but the call would not go through. She threw her phone down on the floor and sobbed. She remembered it all, including her very last memory when both she and Lauren were fleeing back to the ship.

They had just finished their spa treatment and some other girls walked up to them and tried to kiss them. They rejected the kisses and walked away, but as they were leaving, they saw more of these women in a trance staring at them, walking towards them without even speaking. Some smiling.

Lauren and Desiree then broke out into a full on sprint. They passed through the market area and what they saw was an intense scene of widespread orgies and pregnant women. Some with a very large baby struggling on the inside. They got a little further and actually spotted some of the men shrinking down and being swallowed alive. Lauren yelled out, "Xtabay!...It's her curse!"

Desiree tripped and fell, but a pack of the crazed women got on top of her before Lauren could turn around and help. The last thing Desiree saw was Lauren running away screaming as one of her captors crawled over and kissed her. *That must have been when she turned into one of those crazy women! Did she seduce and swallow Charlie like the other women she saw?!*

Then Desiree thought of her vision where she had swallowed Charlie after sex. She quickly stuck her fingers down her throat, almost her whole hand and then bent over in pain as she vomited in the bathtub. From her stomach, through her throat and slowly emerging out of her mouth was a small person, a guy. She carefully regurgitated him onto her open hands and then lowered him into the bathtub. She fell back in shock and almost knew instantly that she had swallowed a person whole.

Then to her surprise the body began to grow back in size all the way to a full grown, man! Desiree almost had a heart attack, possibly several as she watched it all unfold. She then recognized that it was indeed Charlie. *She ate Charlie just as she had daydreamed!* She screamed some more and continued to sob as the reality of it all hit her. Desiree yelled and cursed some more before settling down. She turned on the shower to rinse off the gunk around him and then gave him a gentle hug. Her eyes completely sobbing with tears she leaned in and kissed him.

He was still warm, and his mouth easily parted with her lips, not stiff with rigormortis! She placed her hand next to his neck but didn't feel a pulse. She immediately began CPR.

"Don't you die on me Charlie! Don't you fucking die!" No response.

Minutes go by. Desiree began to think about how Charlie was slowly digesting alive inside of her. Alone and being mashed from all direction with her strong stomach muscles and hot enzymes. How he may have been struggling without any hope of escape.

Then she tried to focus on the positives and thought about what it must have been like while she was seducing and fucking him. She wanted to feel that love with Charlie and not just as a mindless crazed woman, but also as a true lover. She continued CPR to no avail. Finally, Desiree raised up her hand and nearly slapped his face off screaming his name again "CHARLIE!"

"Honestly I just wanted to feel you kiss me several more times Desiree."

"CHARLIE! You MF! How dare!..."

She quickly stopped yelling at him and within seconds, Desiree had grabbed Charlie and picked him out of the bathtub completely. Desiree pulled Charlie deep into her body with a strong bear hug and kissed him. She realized that the wine she had drunk earlier probably slowed down her own metabolism as alcohol was a toxin and the body always tries to metabolize toxins before anything else. Then the oxygenated spa water she followed up with must have increased the oxygen content in her stomach to keep Charlie alive. Charlie's gifts to her saved his own life!

Desiree carried Charlie back over to the bed. She placed him down and crawled right on top with her full body weight again. *Not again, oh please not again.* Charlie thought.

"Don't worry Charlie. I don't bite. I swallow." Charlie's face went pale. *She spit me up only to swallow me down again!...but wait a second, she's still talking to me!*

"I'm joking Charlie! Relax!" Desiree giggled some more and wrapped him up into an intimate snuggle.

She was still very strong. He wondered if this was going to be permanent for her or if she would return to her normal strength. Either way, he was glad that Desiree seemed to have broken free from the curse. *Good thing I put those flowers in her bathroom!*

If it had not been for his discovery of the sweet morning glory flowers in those Mayan ruins he would be a new layer of fat in Desiree's body or perhaps still a soupy mush in her intestines! *What about everyone else? Should they risk trying to bring other crazed girls back from this curse? How could he with only one flower left? How the fuck did this curse start anyway? Shit it was probably when that thing happened to Reina, and what actually happened to her? And...*

It was all so much for him to think through. Charlie cleared his mind and surrendered to Desiree's thick, warm body softly caressing him. He feel asleep as she tightly held onto him, determined not to lose Charlie again.

It was almost sunset and small humming noise began to approach from behind Desiree's balcony. Both Charlie and Desiree peered out to see a large propeller plane flying low and slow towards the ship. As it got close, they could see some type of mist pouring out from its wings. "Gas!" yelled Charlie.

He closed the balcony window door and they both watched the plane fly directly over the ship. Then they heard a helicopter arriving from another direction but could not see it. Once it was hovering over the ship, they heard men jumping onto the boat and yelling.

"ALL SECURE!"

"CONTINUING SWEEP!"

Charlie looked back at Desiree and said, "If we ever get out of this, I'm marrying you."

They quietly turned off all the lights and went back to bed. Desiree climbed on top of him and looked down at Charlie with an eerie look. Then she squeezed her legs around his and pinned his arms to his sides. Just as Charlie was about to freak out, she giggled and released her grip. "Just kidding baby!" she chuckled.

Desiree kissed Charlie sweetly and whispered into his ear, "but you do belong to me now."

She started playing one of her favorite sound tracks on speakerphone, "Kokomo, from the Beach Boys." Then she spread her thighs around his hips and began to ride Charlie into the sunset nice and slow. She was going to take all night with him and then some.

# ABOUT THE AUTHOR

## Jake Adams

Jake Adams is a new erotic artist that focuses on all things related to female vore.  A dark and seductively erotic world where men are devoured alive by sexy women.